SEASIDE CHRISTMAS WISHES

CHRISTMAS SEASHELLS AND SNOWFLAKES

KAY CORRELL

ZURA LU PUBLISHING LLC

Published by Zura Lu Publishing LLC

ABOUT THIS BOOK

A mysterious box of keepsakes holds the key to saving Evie's family cottage—if she can unlock their secrets in time…

When Evie returns to her grandmother's cottage on Belle Island for the first time since her beloved Nana's passing, she uncovers a mysterious box of keepsakes that could unravel her future.

She finds an unexpected ally in the charming neighbor Randy, who shares a special connection to her grandmother's past. Together they begin unraveling the secrets and heartwarming stories behind each keepsake, awakening Evie's dream of honoring her grandmother's legacy by making the cottage her home.

As Christmas nears, she discovers more than she ever imagined—a gift of new beginnings, rekindled love, and a chance to finally embrace the cherished island life her grandmother loved.

But a surprise visitor makes a

shocking claim that could cost Evie the very cottage she loves.

Will the magic of the season and the power of community be enough to save the cottage and Evie's chance at happiness?

Seaside Christmas Wishes is a heartwarming story of family, love, and the enduring charm of a coastal Christmas. Full of warmth, whimsical surprises, and the enchanting spirit of Christmas, *Seaside Christmas Wishes* is a life-affirming novel about treasuring the past, embracing the present, and having the courage to make your own future.

Christmas Seashells and Snowflakes is a series of holiday books, each a stand-alone story. They are set in some of the locations my readers have come to love, with special appearances of some of my favorite characters. *The books in this series can be read in any order.*

KAY'S BOOKS

Find more information on all my books at
kaycorrell.com
Buy direct from Kay's Shop at
shop.kaycorrell.com

COMFORT CROSSING ~ THE SERIES

The Shop on Main - Book One
The Memory Box - Book Two
The Christmas Cottage - A Holiday Novella (Book 2.5)
The Letter - Book Three
The Christmas Scarf - A Holiday Novella (Book 3.5)
The Magnolia Cafe - Book Four
The Unexpected Wedding - Book Five

The Wedding in the Grove - (a crossover short story between series - with Josephine and Paul from The Letter.)

LIGHTHOUSE POINT ~ THE SERIES

Wish Upon a Shell - Book One
Wedding on the Beach - Book Two
Love at the Lighthouse - Book Three
Cottage near the Point - Book Four
Return to the Island - Book Five
Bungalow by the Bay - Book Six
Christmas Comes to Lighthouse Point - Book Seven

CHARMING INN ~ Return to Lighthouse Point

One Simple Wish - Book One
Two of a Kind - Book Two
Three Little Things - Book Three
Four Short Weeks - Book Four
Five Years or So - Book Five
Six Hours Away - Book Six
Charming Christmas - Book Seven

SWEET RIVER ~ THE SERIES

A Dream to Believe in - Book One
A Memory to Cherish - Book Two

A Song to Remember - Book Three
A Time to Forgive - Book Four
A Summer of Secrets - Book Five
A Moment in the Moonlight - Book Six

MOONBEAM BAY ~ THE SERIES

The Parker Women - Book One
The Parker Cafe - Book Two
A Heather Parker Original - Book Three
The Parker Family Secret - Book Four
Grace Parker's Peach Pie - Book Five
The Perks of Being a Parker - Book Six

BLUE HERON COTTAGES ~ THE SERIES

Memories of the Beach - Book One
Walks along the Shore - Book Two
Bookshop near the Coast - Book Three
Restaurant on the Wharf - Book Four
Lilacs by the Sea - Book Five
Flower Shop on Magnolia - Book Six
Christmas by the Bay - Book Seven
Sea Glass from the Past - Book Eight

MAGNOLIA KEY ~ THE SERIES

Saltwater Sunrise - Book One
Encore Echoes - Book Two

Coastal Candlelight - Book Three
Tidal Treasures - Book Four
And more to come!

CHRISTMAS SEASHELLS AND SNOWFLAKES
Seaside Christmas Wishes

WIND CHIME BEACH ~ A stand-alone novel

INDIGO BAY ~
Sweet Days by the Bay - Kay's Complete Collection of stories in the Indigo Bay series

Sign up for my newsletter at my website *kaycorrell.com* to make sure you don't miss any new releases or sales.

This book is dedicated to my mother. She made the Christmas season a very special time for our family. My boys have carried on with so many of her traditions.

Mom, I wish you were here for Clara's first Christmas. You'd fall hopelessly in love with her like I have.

CHAPTER 1

Evie's heart quickened as she drove over the bridge to Belle Island. The familiar shoreline came into view, a mix of sandy beaches and weathered docks that stirred a bittersweet ache in her chest. She hadn't visited in years. Now she was returning to a place that held so many cherished memories but without her beloved Nana—the woman who had made them all possible.

She rolled down the window and let the salty breeze tousle her hair, carrying with it the scent of sea grass and sun-warmed sand. Evie took in a deep breath and let the sensations wash over her. It was as if time had stood still here, preserving every detail of her childhood summers spent exploring the island with her grandmother.

She drove through the familiar—yet not so familiar—streets of the town. How many years had it been since she'd been back? Ten? Fifteen? More? Her life had gotten so hectic and it had gotten harder and harder to make time to come visit.

Her grandmother had visited her often, though. They always had the best time together. Until the last visit. The one when Nana had gotten sick and ended up in the hospital. She'd died there, never getting the chance to return to her beloved Belle Island.

As she drove around the island, the Christmas decorations declared the town's enthusiastic embrace of the season. Twinkle lights in the store windows. Wreaths and bright red bows hung on the lampposts. The festiveness mocked the heavy sadness that clung to her every moment.

She turned onto Nana's street and as the cottage came into view, she slowed the car. The weathered blue shutters, the white picket fence that was always kept freshly painted, the creaky porch swing—it was all exactly as she remembered. But, of course, now it was all different, changed. The warmth of her grandmother's presence was missing, leaving the cottage feeling hollow despite its familiar exterior.

Evie pulled into the driveway, the crushed shell crunching beneath her tires. Once parked, she grabbed a bag from the back seat and headed up the porch stairs. Her hand trembled slightly as she inserted the key into the lock. The metal was cool against her skin as she turned the key, hearing the familiar click of the lock, and pushed the door open.

The scent of lavender and old books surrounded her the moment she stepped inside. Her breath caught in her throat as she took in the entryway. Her grandmother's favorite shawl hung on the coat rack as if waiting for Nana to return from a quick errand. Framed photographs lined the walls, moments frozen in time—her gap-toothed grin on her sixth birthday, and Nana's proud smile at her college graduation.

Overwhelmed, she leaned against the doorframe, tears forming in the corners of her eyes. The realization that her grandmother was truly gone hit her anew, the pain as fresh as the day she'd sat by Nana's side, watching her last breaths.

After a moment, she straightened and began to move through the cottage. Each room held an overwhelming amount of treasured memories. In the kitchen, she ran her fingers along the worn countertop where she and Nana baked countless batches of Christmas cookies. The old recipe box still sat in its place of honor, filled with handwritten cards bearing the secrets to Nana's culinary magic.

The living room was stuffed full of memories of cozy evenings spent reading on the couch—Nana had instilled in her a love of reading—or playing board games during summer storms. Her gaze lingered on her grandmother's favorite armchair, the floral upholstery faded but still inviting. She could almost hear her grandmother's laughter and picture her settled comfortably in the chair, her ever-present knitting bag nestled at her side. She swore she could hear the needles softly clicking together as Nana's fingers moved in the familiar, almost hypnotic rhythm of her latest knitting project.

As she turned from the front room and made her way upstairs, each creaky step echoed through the quiet house. She paused at the door to her old room, hesitating for just a moment before pushing it open. Inside, it was as if she had never left. The same quilted bedspread, the shelf of well-loved books, even the collection of seashells she had gathered over countless summers—all were exactly as she had left them years ago.

She sat on the edge of the bed, running her hand over the soft fabric of the quilt. The room felt smaller now, yet it still held the same sense of safety and love that had always defined her visits to Belle Island. As she looked around, taking in every familiar detail, a mixture of grief, nostalgia, and an unexpected sense of homecoming swept through her.

She dropped her bag in the room and crossed the hall to her grandmother's room, her heart catching in her chest. The same chenille bedspread stretched across the bed with the same faded throw pillows resting against the headboard. She wandered over to the dresser and picked up the bottle of Nana's favorite perfume. She sprayed some on her wrist and inhaled, closing her eyes and getting lost in the familiar scent.

She sucked in a deep breath, steadying

herself as she left the room and headed back downstairs. Memories of sliding down the smooth banister as a child flashed through her mind as she trailed her fingers along it. When she reached the bottom, her glance caught a crisp white envelope sitting on the hall table.

The return address bore the name of her grandmother's lawyer. She picked up the envelope, its weight feeling far heavier than it should. She slid her finger under the flap, tearing it open carefully.

Inside, she found two folded sheets of paper. The first was a formal letter from the lawyer, but it was the second that made her breath catch. She recognized her grandmother's elegant handwriting immediately. Her eyes welled with tears as she unfolded the letter and began to read:

My dearest Evie,

If you're reading this, it means I am gone. I hope you'll forgive me for the surprise, but I wanted to leave you with these words, knowing they'd reach you when you needed them most.

First, let me say how proud I am of you. You've grown into a remarkable woman, full of strength and kindness. I've watched you blossom from afar, wishing I could be there for every moment, but knowing you needed to spread your wings. As I always said, we end up in life where we're supposed to be.

I know coming back to Belle Island without me here will be difficult. This place holds so many memories for both of us. But I hope you'll find comfort in those memories, and perhaps make some new ones.

The cottage is yours now, my dear. It's been in our family for generations, and I can think of no one better to care for it. I hope it can be a special place for you, just as it has been for me all these years. A place where you can come and rest and heal when you need to.

There's so much more I want to tell you, but I'll save that for another letter. For now, know that I love you, always have, and always will. You were named after me, but you've made the name Evie entirely your own.

Take care of yourself, my sweet girl. And remember, no matter where you are, a piece of Belle Island will always be with you, as will I.

All my love,

Nana

Her vision blurred as tears spilled onto her cheeks. She clutched the letter to her chest, her grandmother's words wrapping around her almost as if Nana was here hugging her.

She reread the letter, hearing her grandmother's voice in her head as clearly as if she were standing right beside her. Dashing away her tears, she looked around the entryway with fresh eyes. The cottage wasn't just a cottage filled with memories. It was so much more. It was a gift, a legacy. Nana's love and spirit infused every nook and cranny.

She walked to the living room window, gazing out at the familiar view of the shoreline. The sun was beginning to set, painting the sky in soft pinks and oranges. A lone blue heron stalked along the shoreline with long, ambling steps. As she stood there, letter still in hand, Evie felt a small shift within herself. The pain of loss was still there, but alongside it was a sense of belonging, of being where she was supposed to be. At least for now.

CHAPTER 2

The next morning, Evie awoke to the soft light filtering through the blinds of her room in Nana's cottage. She stretched and yawned, her mind still heavy with sleep. She sat up slowly and smiled, taking in the comforting surroundings that held so many memories.

Downstairs, she padded barefoot into the kitchen and reached for the coffee canister on the counter, only to find it empty. Disappointment floated through her. She'd need to head into town for groceries and, most importantly, coffee.

She picked up her phone and quickly searched for the nearest grocery shop. A smile tugged at her lips when she discovered that every Saturday, there was an outdoor market in the heart of town. And, lucky her, today was Saturday.

Energized by the prospect of fresh produce and local delicacies, she quickly got dressed and grabbed a few cloth bags. As she stepped outside, the warm sea air caressed her, carrying with it a hint of salt and the distant cries of seagulls.

She paused for a moment, breathing in the scent of the blooming flowers in Nana's garden. Nana always made sure something was in bloom all year round. The colorful blossoms swayed in the breeze, proof of her grandmother's love and care.

She set off down the sidewalk toward town. The sun warmed her skin as she walked. Most of the cottages had Christmas decorations adorning their porches. But she wasn't here to celebrate the holidays. She was here to sort through Nana's things and figure out what to do with the cottage. The decorations were just a reminder that she was all alone this Christmas. Christmas was the one holiday that she'd always celebrated with Nana, even if the last ones had been in Baltimore at her place. Nana made sure to come every year so Evie wouldn't be alone.

Trying to ignore the cheerful decorations, she approached the market. Stalls lined the streets, each one offering a bounty of fresh fruits, vegetables, baked goods, and handmade crafts. It all was enticing, but first things first. She went to the coffee booth and bought a large coffee.

Sipping her coffee, she browsed the offerings, marveling at the vibrant colors and fragrant aromas. The choices were a bit overwhelming. As she moved from stall to stall, she found herself drawn to a display of handmade pottery. The pieces were beautiful, each one unique and crafted with care. She ran her fingers over a mug glazed in a soft shade of blue, admiring the artisan's work.

"That's one of my favorites," a voice said from behind the table. Evie looked up to see a woman with kind eyes and silver hair smiling at her. "I made it with the colors of the sea in mind."

She smiled back, instantly warmed by the woman's friendly smile. "It's beautiful," she said, picking up the mug and cradling it in her hands. "I'll take it."

As the woman wrapped the mug in tissue paper, Evie felt a sense of connection to the island again. It was as if a piece of her grandmother's spirit lived on with her as she walked the streets of Belle Island.

As she navigated the vibrant stalls overflowing with fresh produce and homemade goods, the tantalizing scents of freshly baked bread and ripe fruit made her mouth water. She paused at a stall displaying an array of local honey, the golden jars gleaming in the sunlight. She hadn't had honey in forever, but Nana had always kept some. She would make homemade croissants and drizzle honey over them and used honey to sweeten her hot tea and her oatmeal.

Reaching for a particularly appealing jar tied with a gingham ribbon, her hand froze mid-air as another hand reached for it at the same moment. She looked up to see a man with sun-weathered skin and kind eyes. He smiled warmly at her, his eyes crinkling at the corners in a friendly manner.

"Sorry about that," he said in a deep, pleasant voice. "Please, you take it."

She returned his smile, grateful for his graciousness. "Thank you. That's very kind of you," she said, picking up the jar and cradling it in her hands. "I'm Eve, by the way. I'm just visiting the island."

The man's smile widened, and a hint of pride filled his chestnut-brown eyes. "Welcome to Belle Island, Evie. I'm Randy, and I've lived here my whole life. It's a special place."

She felt an instant connection to him, his friendly smile putting her at ease. "It really is," she agreed, glancing around at the market.

"Seeing that you're new here, would you like me to show you around the market? I'll show you the best stalls for everything," he offered.

"Oh, I'd love that, thank you. I admit I'm a bit overwhelmed with it all. I barely know where to start."

"Except for the honey." He grinned at her.

"Except for that."

As they strolled through the market, Randy's enthusiasm for the island was infectious. He guided her to various stalls, pointing out the best produce and unique items each vendor had to offer.

"Over here, you'll find the freshest seafood caught by our local fishermen," he said, gesturing to a stall displaying an array of fish and shellfish on beds of ice. "And if you're looking for the perfect loaf of sourdough, you can't go wrong with Julie's bread. She owns The Sweet Shoppe in town."

She followed his lead, marveling at the quality and variety of the goods. She sampled a slice of tangy sourdough and savored the burst of flavor from a perfectly ripe strawberry.

As they walked, they chatted about the island's history and the close-knit community that called it home. Randy shared stories of growing up on Belle Island, painting a picture of a place where everyone looked out for one another. "The kind of place where you can always count on your neighbors," he said with a smile. "If you ever need anything, just ask. Someone will be happy to help."

She nodded, thinking of how her grandmother had always spoken fondly of the island's friendly residents and how helpful they were to each other.

They paused at a stall selling handmade jewelry, and she admired the delicate seashell earrings and sea glass pendants. Randy picked up a pair of earrings and held them up to her ears.

"These would look lovely on you," he said, his eyes twinkling. "The blue matches your eyes perfectly."

She blushed, surprised by the compliment.

She couldn't remember the last time someone had noticed the color of her eyes.

Before she knew it, they'd reached the end of the market. Randy turned to her with a warm smile. "Well, that's the grand tour," he said. "I hope you enjoyed it as much as I did."

Evie grinned, feeling a genuine connection to both the island and its friendly inhabitants. "It was wonderful. Thank you for showing me around."

"It was my pleasure," he replied. "If you ever need anything, just ask. Everyone is always willing to help here on the island."

"I'll keep that in mind. Thank you again."

With a final wave, Randy disappeared into the crowd. She stood for a moment, basking in the warmth of the sun as memories of times here with her Nana flitted through her mind. Why had she not made it a point to come back here every year? Instead, she'd always insisted she was so busy that Nana had to make the trip to come see her.

As she walked back toward Nana's cottage, she realized she wasn't here just to organize her grandmother's possessions but also to rekindle her connection to the island. The one she'd had when she was younger and her parents would send her to the island each summer. After her parents died when she was in college, Nana made sure that Evie spent every Christmas with her, never leaving her alone.

Until this year.

CHAPTER 3

That evening, Evie stood at the edge of the shore, her feet sinking into the cool sand as the sun began to set, painting the sky in vibrant oranges, pinks, and purples. The gentle lapping of waves against the shoreline created a soothing rhythm over her feet. Breathing deeply, she savored the salty sea air even as she wrapped her arms around herself against the evening breeze.

She gazed out at the horizon, and memories of long walks on this very beach with Nana flooded her mind—collecting seashells, building sandcastles, and watching the sunset together. A bittersweet smile played on her lips as she recalled how Nana would always say, "The sky's putting on a show just for us, Evie-girl."

The ache of loss mingled with the warmth of happy memories, leaving her feeling both comforted and melancholy. She wondered what Nana would say if she could see her now, standing on their favorite stretch of beach, trying to find her way forward without Nana's guidance.

As she stood there, lost in her thoughts, she looked down the beach and saw a lone figure approaching in the dimming light.

As the person drew closer, she recognized Randy from their encounter at the market earlier that day. His tall frame and easy gait were unmistakable, even in the fading light. She felt a blend of surprise and curiosity at seeing him again so soon, wondering what he was doing on this stretch of beach.

"Evening, Eve," Randy called out as he came within earshot, his voice carrying on the sea breeze. "Fancy meeting you out here. It's a beautiful night out, isn't it?"

"Randy, hi." She tucked a strand of hair behind her ear. "It is a beautiful night. I was just out watching the sunset."

"Looks like the sky's putting on a show just for us." He motioned toward the sunset.

Her eyes widened in surprise, and a gasp

escaped her lips. "Oh, my Nana used to say that very thing to me."

He looked at her closely, his brow creasing. "Are you Miss Genevieve's granddaughter? Evie?"

"I am." She turned and motioned to the cottage. "I'm here trying to sort out her things."

"Oh, I'm so sorry for your loss." His voice softened with genuine sympathy. "Miss G was a wonderful person."

"You knew her?"

"I did. I'm her neighbor." He pointed to the cottage next to Nana's. "I moved to the cottage about ten years ago, although I've lived on the island my whole life. Your grandmother and I had some great times together. She'd always bring plates of cookies she made or ask me over for dinner. We lost a great woman."

"We did."

"I'm surprised I haven't met you before. But your grandmother spoke of you often. I should have realized it was you when you told me your name was Eve, although Miss G always called you Evie."

"I... I haven't been here in a very long time. Life got... crazy." Like her longtime boyfriend who hated for her to leave town and a demanding job. Neither of which she had anymore. Luckily, she'd responsibly saved her earnings and had a bit of money inherited from Nana, hopefully enough to tide her over until she got her feet back under her.

"You going to keep the cottage? Miss G said that she was leaving it to you."

She looked at him for a long moment and shrugged. "I don't know. I mean, I still have my place in the city. It seems a bit silly to keep both places."

"It would be hard to give up that cottage. Your grandmother made it such a welcoming place, and it has a great view."

"I know. And it holds so many memories. But… it's not the same without Nana here with me." A pang of loss filtered through her.

His eyes filled with understanding. "I'm sure it's not." He reached out and lightly touched her arm. "If you need any help with anything, please just ask. I'm sure it's an overwhelming job to sort through her things."

"I have to admit, I haven't even started. Avoiding it, I guess. Just wanted to get settled in first." She squared her shoulders. "But I'm going to start into it tomorrow. And I should probably head in. It's getting dark."

He walked her to the steps to her deck. "Good night, then. And my offer stands. I can help if you need me." He paused. "Or… if you just need someone to talk to."

"Thank you. Good night." She climbed the stairs and stood on the deck, taking one last look at the water stretching before her. A slice of moonlight illuminated the waves. She glanced over toward Randy's cottage, where warm light spilled out from his windows. It was nice to know someone here on the island. It made her feel not quite so alone.

Randy stood in his kitchen drinking a large glass of ice water, looking out the window toward Miss G's cottage. Well, he guessed it was Evie's cottage now if she decided to keep it.

The look in Evie's eyes when she talked about her grandmother… so much pain. But then, he remembered that pain from when his own grandmother passed away. A hole in his heart that he thought he'd never get over. The pain lessened over the years but never fully went away.

To be honest, he felt Miss G's passing almost

as much as he had his own grandmother's. He'd moved into the cottage next to hers after a nasty divorce where his wife had just up and left him but wanted everything in the divorce settlement.

He'd known Miss G from living here on the island, of course. Everyone knew everybody. But he'd gotten close to her after moving next door. She'd found him one day sitting on the beach right after he moved in, wallowing in the shock and pain of his divorce and the sense of betrayal. Miss G had sat silently beside him for a bit, then reached out and took his hand. "It's hard to lose someone, no matter the circumstances. It upends your life with changes. But you're going to be okay. I promise. It does get easier."

And that had started their friendship. He fixed things at her cottage for her and she brought food over to him often, claiming she'd made too much for just herself. They often sat and watched the sunsets together. And he couldn't even count how many glasses of sweet tea he'd had sitting over on her porch.

Fate had thrown them together, and an unexpected and much-appreciated friendship had grown between them. He cherished the memories of their time together and felt a loss with her gone, no longer able to just pop in and see her.

Evie must be feeling that loss just as acutely. And he'd had two chance meetings with Evie today. First at the market and then on the beach tonight. What were the chances? He wouldn't put it past Miss G if she were orchestrating this from beyond. Making sure someone was there checking on her granddaughter, knowing he would understand what she was going through.

He'd do just that for Miss G. Check on Evie. Reiterate his offer to help her go through her grandmother's things. It's the least he could do after all that Miss G had done for him.

CHAPTER 4

The next morning, Evie made her way to the kitchen, her bare feet padding softly across the worn wooden floors. She ran her hand along the familiar countertop, feeling the smooth surface beneath her fingertips. The kitchen looked just as she remembered it from her childhood summers—the cheerful yellow curtains, the collection of mismatched mugs, the old teal wall clock. She was surprised to see that Nana had replaced the old percolator she had used every morning without fail. In its place was a shiny, stainless-steel drip coffee maker.

She hunted around until she found the filters and filled the coffeemaker with water and coffee grounds. As the coffee brewed, she breathed in the rich aroma that filled the kitchen, closing her eyes for a moment to savor the memories it evoked.

Cup in hand, she stepped out onto the porch and settled into one of the weathered rocking chairs. She sipped her coffee slowly, watching the morning unfold on the island. A few early risers strolled along the beach, their dogs trotting beside them. In the distance, she could see a boat heading out for a day of fishing.

The scene before her stirred up memories of countless mornings spent here with her grandmother. They would sit side by side, Nana telling stories of the island's history or sharing wisdom gleaned from her years of living by the sea. Her grandmother had moved to the island when she married Evie's grandfather. He'd died when Evie was young, so she barely remembered him. All the trips to the island she remembered were just her and Nana. Her own parents always seemed grateful to ship her off to the island for the summer, busy with their jobs and life.

Finishing her coffee, Evie took a deep breath and stood up. It was time to face the task she'd avoided since her arrival—sorting through her grandmother's belongings. She headed back inside, pausing in the hallway to look at the family photos that lined the walls. There was one of her as a little girl, building a sandcastle with Nana. Another showed her parents on their wedding day with a young Genevieve beaming proudly beside them.

She trudged into the living room with slow steps. She stood in the center of the room for a moment, taking in the familiar surroundings. Her grandmother's presence lingered in every corner—in the handmade knitted throw draped over the back of the sofa, in the collection of seashells arranged on the mantel, and in the faint scent of lavender that still hung in the air.

With a small sigh, she began her task. She started with the bookshelf, carefully removing each book and deciding whether to keep it or donate it. Some choices were easy—the well-worn copy of *Heidi* that Nana had read to her every summer was an immediate keeper. Oh, and *Little Women*, the pages wrinkled with time and numerous readings. Others were more difficult, each holding a memory or story that made it hard to part with.

When it became too difficult to keep making decisions about the books, she moved on to Nana's storage closet. She opened the door and pulled the string and the line of bare lightbulbs popped on, illuminating the shelves lining the walls.

She walked into the closet and reached for a small, dusty box tucked away on one of the shelves. As she pulled it out, she realized it was filled with postcards and letters—the very ones she'd sent to Nana over the years. A lump formed in her throat as she gently lifted the stack of correspondence tied neatly with a faded ribbon. Proof that Nana had treasured every word, every memory Evie had shared with her, preserving them like precious heirlooms.

She carefully untied the ribbon and began to leaf through the postcards and letters. Each one transported her back to a specific moment in time—a childhood summer spent exploring the island, a teenage heartbreak she had confided to Nana, a college triumph she couldn't wait to share. She marveled at the way her grandmother had lovingly kept these pieces of her life, a record of their bond.

With a bittersweet ache in her chest, she placed the stack of letters back in the box, making a mental note to read through them more thoroughly later. She moved further into the storage closet, past the neatly labeled boxes of Christmas decorations. Nana had always gone all out for the holidays, transforming the cottage into a winter wonderland filled with twinkling lights, garlands, and the scent of freshly baked cookies. That wouldn't be the way it was this year, she reminded herself.

As she reached the back of the closet, she pushed aside a few boxes to reveal a small wooden box she had never seen before. The lid was adorned with an intricate Christmas design, the carved details worn smooth with age. Curious what treasures her grandmother had hidden away, she carefully lifted the lid.

She held it under the light and peeked inside. The box held an assortment of items, each one wrapped in tissue paper. She settled the lid back on the box and set it by the closet door to take it out later and go through it in better light.

Turning back to the task at hand, she found she just didn't have it in her to continue. She couldn't bear to open the Christmas boxes and see the familiar decorations Nana put out each year. The light-up ceramic Christmas tree with its tiny little lights. A set of three carved wooden caroling mice, of all things. A Christmas angel that spun around on a stand while the tones of

"Silent Night" filled the cottage. No, she couldn't go there. Not yet.

She turned, scooped up the wooden box, and resolutely pulled the chain, plunging the closet into darkness. She headed out to the living room and set the box down, looking at the bookshelves. Yet another job she hadn't finished.

Deciding to give herself a little grace, she decided to take a break. She hadn't been to the lighthouse since her return. It was one of her favorite places on the island. Nana had totally believed in the town legend that if you stood at Lighthouse Point, made a wish, and threw a shell into the sea, your wish would come true.

But first, she needed a hat—her grandmother was big on wearing hats in the sun and had a huge collection of them. Her grandmother's closet still smelled of Nana—a mix of lavender and her grandmother's favorite perfume. She buried her face in Nana's favorite robe, savoring the scent, remembering how if she ever got sick in the summer, Nana would plop her on the couch and cover her with the robe, insisting it would make her better.

She turned and looked at the shelves filled with hats. With a smile, she pulled out a perky straw hat and placed it on her head. She could almost feel Nana's approval.

Once outside, she headed down to the water's edge, walking along the foamy remains of the waves. As she approached the lighthouse, she admired the familiar building standing guard over the island as it had for so many years.

She stood beneath the lighthouse, looking out to sea, the moment familiar and yet so different without Nana by her side. She bent down and picked up a delicate shell with traces of pink on it, then wrapped her fist around it and closed her eyes.

She made her wish, opened her eyes, and tossed the shell out into the water, watching it disappear beneath the surface. Not that she believed her wish would come true.

CHAPTER 5

Evie woke up the next morning, momentarily confused as to where she was. Then she remembered. Nana's. The silence of the cottage surrounded her. There was no sound of Nana's cheerful humming or bustling movements coming from the kitchen.

She slid out of bed, determined to shake off the melancholy that threatened to settle over her. A sudden thought popped into her mind. Why not go out for breakfast? She could see if Magic Cafe was still here. She'd loved going there with Nana. And the cafe was always filled with people, and chatter, and laughter. Just what she needed right now.

She slipped on shorts, a T-shirt, and sandals

and headed to the cafe, pleased to find it still here after all her years away.

Pushing open the door, she was greeted by the comforting aroma of freshly brewed coffee and baked goods. The interior was just as she remembered—cozy and inviting, with a touch of coastal charm in its decor. Tally, the owner, stood behind the counter and looked up as she approached.

"Good morning. Welcome to Magic Cafe." Tally smiled at her, then the dawning of recognition spread across her face. "Evie? Is that you?"

"Yes, it's me." She grinned at the fact that Tally still recognized her.

"Evie, dear, it's so good to see you." Tally came around and wrapped her in a big hug. "Oh, honey, I was so sorry to hear about Genevieve. She was such a special lady."

Tears crept into the corners of her eyes and she wondered if she was ever going to be able to hear about Nana or talk about her without tears threatening to fall. A lump formed in her throat at Tally's kind words. The genuine compassion in Tally's expression comforted her grieving heart. She offered a grateful smile in return. "Thank you. She was special. And

Nana loved to come here. It feels good to be back."

"You come on in. I'll get you a table right by the beach, just like you always liked."

"Thanks, Tally." She followed her out across the wooden deck to a table near the edge of the beach. As she settled into her seat, the clink of coffee mugs and murmured conversations filled the air around her. The gentle hum of life in the cafe wrapped around her, grounding her in the present moment.

She glanced at all the Christmas decorations on the railings and twinkle lights hung from the ceilings. Tally noticed her perusal and grinned. "Yep, still go a bit overboard for Christmas."

"It looks great." Looks familiar. Just like she remembered. And the familiarity was comforting.

Tally poured her a cup of coffee and handed her a menu. "Menu is mostly the same. We don't like change much around here."

"I'm finding I don't like change either." She took the menu from Tally.

"I'll be back in a flash to get your order. Then I think I'll sit down with you if you don't mind and we'll catch up."

"I'd like that."

She ordered an omelet and hash browns, and soon Tally brought it out and sat across from her.

"Feels good to sit down for a bit," Tally said as she took a sip of coffee. "So, tell me what's new with you."

"I'm here to deal with all of Nana's things. I admit, it's a bit overwhelming. I'm not making much progress."

"There's no hurry to it, is there?"

"Well, if I want to get it on the market, I'll need to clear it out."

"You selling it?" Tally raised her eyebrow. "I just figured you'd keep it as a vacation place, if nothing else."

"I don't really need two places, and I have my condo back in Baltimore."

"I guess you do need to get back to your job."

She sighed. "Not really. I got let go." Lost Nana, let go from her job, and her boyfriend dropped her, all in a two-week span.

"I'm sorry. But I'm sure you'll find a new one lickety-split. Genevieve was always bragging about the promotions you were getting."

"Hope so. But I have to admit, this little break from… well, from everything is nice. And it's nice to be back on Belle Island, even under these circumstances."

"We're glad to have you back." Tally reached over and patted her hand. "So, how's the sorting out of the cottage going?"

"It's a lot to handle. And I found the most interesting thing in Nana's storage closet. A wooden box with a Christmas design carved on top. It has a bunch of wrapped items in it. I'm not sure where they're from or why she had them."

Tally shrugged. "I've sure got no clue. But they must have been special to her for her to keep them."

"I should unwrap them and see if I can figure out why she had them all tucked away like that."

"You could ask Randy, your neighbor. He and Genevieve were great friends."

"Oh, I met him. He helped me out at the market, then we talked for a bit last night."

"He's a nice man. Lived here all his life. He's really into island history, too. He and Genevieve were always researching something or other. Randy volunteers at the historical society."

"Thank you. I'll talk to him."

Tally stood. "Well, I better get back to work. I hope you come back often. It's great seeing you."

"I'm sure I'll be back soon."

Tally walked away, stopping to talk to each table on her way back toward the kitchen. Not much had changed here at Magic Cafe, and she liked that. She needed some stability in her life right now.

Evie walked down the sandy path toward Randy's cottage, the wooden box tucked under her arm. It was impossible not to notice the festive atmosphere surrounding his home. Strings of colorful Christmas lights were draped along the deck railing, twinkling in the early evening light. Randy, perched precariously on a stepladder, was in the process of hanging yet another strand when he spotted her. He waved enthusiastically, nearly losing his balance in the process.

"Whoa there," she called out, quickening her pace. "Don't go falling on my account."

He chuckled, regaining his footing. "I've got it under control. Trust me."

She walked up to the base of the old wooden ladder and wasn't entirely certain she believed him. She set the box down. "Here, let me hold this steady for you. Don't need you taking a tumble."

"Thanks." He grinned down at her, his eyes crinkling at the corners. "I appreciate the help."

As he continued to string the lights, she glanced around at the abundance of decorations already in place. Wreaths hung on the windows, and a large reindeer made out of a split log adorned the edge of his deck. "You really go all out for Christmas, don't you?"

"I haven't hardly started yet. There's still the tree. Two, actually. One out here on the deck and one inside." He grinned again. "It's a tradition I've maintained ever since I moved into this cottage. Have to keep up with Miss G's decorations, you know? She always had the most festive place on the island."

She nodded, surprised that the mention of Nana didn't bring the usual fight with tears, and instead, a feeling of nostalgia swept through her. "Nana did love Christmas. I remember helping her decorate when I was a kid. We'd spend hours untangling lights and hanging ornaments."

"She had a way of making everything feel magical," Randy said, climbing down the ladder. "I always admired that about her."

"Me too." She picked up the wooden box, running her fingers over the intricate Christmas design of wreaths and holly carved into the lid. "Speaking of Nana, I actually came over to ask you about something I found in her storage closet."

His eyebrows rose in interest. "Oh? What did you find?"

She held out the box. "This. It's filled with wrapped items, but I have no idea where they came from or what they mean. I've never seen the box before. Tally mentioned that you and Nana were close, so I thought maybe you might know something about it."

He took the box and shook his head. "I've never seen this before, but it definitely looks like something Miss G would have treasured." He glanced up at her. "Why don't we go inside and take a closer look? I need to take a break, anyway."

"I don't want to stop you from your decorating extravaganza." She grinned at him.

"Oh, you're not. I promise you the

decorating will continue. For days." He winked at her. "It's just what I do."

CHAPTER 6

Evie followed Randy into his cottage and was immediately struck by the cozy atmosphere. The interior was filled with warm, inviting colors and well-loved furniture. It felt lived-in and comfortable, much like Nana's place next door. As she glanced around the room, her gaze landed on a series of framed photographs displayed on a nearby shelf.

She stepped closer and examined the images more carefully. To her surprise, many of the photos featured Randy and Nana together, smiling and laughing in various island locations. In one picture, they were seated on a bench near the lighthouse, the sun setting behind them. Another showed them at the annual Belle Island Christmas Festival, both wearing festive

—and ridiculous-looking—sweaters and holding steaming mugs of cocoa.

"I had no idea you and Nana were so close," she said softly, turning to face him.

He smiled, a hint of nostalgia in his eyes. "Your grandmother was an extraordinary woman. She welcomed me with open arms when I first moved in here, back when I was going through a rough patch in my life. I'd known her before that, but… well, we became good friends after becoming neighbors."

She settled onto the couch, her curiosity aroused. "What do you mean?"

He sank into a nearby armchair, leaning forward slightly. "I moved to this cottage…" He paused for a moment, and a flicker of something flitted through his eyes. He cleared his throat. "I moved here after my wife left me. I admit, I was lost, and I was angry. Miss G saw I was struggling and took me under her wing. Assured me I'd get through everything and I'd be all right."

He chuckled softly, shaking his head. "She'd invite me over for coffee and homemade croissants with honey drizzled over them, or sometimes, sweet tea and cookies. We'd spend hours talking about everything under the sun. The weather, the news, town gossip." He shrugged. "She had a way of making me feel like I belonged, and like everything was going to be okay. And you know what? After a while… it was."

A lump formed in her throat as she listened to his story. She'd always known that Nana was a kind and generous person, but hearing about this side of her life—the way she had been there for Randy during a difficult time—reaffirmed everything she believed about what a good person Nana was.

It was a surprise, of course, to learn about this unexpected friendship that she never knew existed. But there was also a growing sense of connection to Randy, a feeling that they shared something special through their love for Nana.

"She never mentioned any of this to me," she said quietly, glancing back at the photographs. "I had no idea you two were so close, but I'm happy you were. That you were there for her, and she was there for you."

He nodded slowly. "Your grandmother was a private person in many ways. She didn't like to burden others with her own troubles or the struggles of those she cared about. But she was always there, always ready to lend an ear or a helping hand."

She nodded, understanding dawning on her. It was just like Nana to keep something like this to herself, to offer support and love without seeking recognition or praise. "I'm glad you two became friends," she said, meeting his gaze. "It means a lot to know that Nana had someone like you in her life, someone who appreciated her as much as I did."

He reached out, placing a hand on her shoulder. "She loved you more than anything, Evie. Never doubt that. And I know she'd be so proud of the woman you've become."

She blinked back tears, the warmth of his words washing over her. In that moment, sitting in his cozy living room surrounded by memories of Nana, she felt a sense of peace that she hadn't experienced in a long time.

Randy laughed and broke the seriousness of the moment. "I don't suppose you were buying that honey at the market because you know how to make those croissants that Miss G was so famous for."

"It might have been the very reason I allowed you to be so gracious and let me have that jar I wanted."

He gave her an impish grin. "Good decision on my part, then, wasn't it?"

"I could probably make it worth your while." She laughed. "If I still remember how to make them."

He stood. "How about I make us some hot cocoa? I know it's warm here on the island, but the Christmas season just seems to call for hot cocoa."

"I wouldn't say no to that."

He returned after a few minutes with two steaming mugs of hot cocoa. She took a sip of the rich, creamy hot chocolate, savoring the warmth and comfort it provided. The sweet aroma mingled with the scent of Randy's cottage, creating a cozy atmosphere that felt both familiar and new.

"How about we look at this box now, shall we?" Randy set his mug down and reached for the box, carefully lifting the lid. Inside, an assortment of items were nestled in tissue paper, each one wrapped with care. He handed her the first package, a small, delicately wrapped bundle.

She gently peeled back the layers of tissue, revealing a stunning Christmas ornament. The hand-blown glass caught the light, sending shimmering reflections dancing across the room. The ornament was a work of art, with intricate swirls of color and delicate patterns etched into the surface.

"This is beautiful," she breathed, holding it up to admire the craftsmanship.

Randy leaned closer, studying the ornament with a thoughtful expression. "You know, I remember this one. Miss G had it hanging on her Christmas tree every year. She told me it was made by a local artisan, someone named Sam. I can't quite recall his last name, though."

Evie turned the ornament over in her hands, marveling at the attention to detail. The fact that Nana had cherished this piece, displaying it prominently on her tree, made it all the more special. She could almost picture her grandmother carefully unwrapping the ornament each year, a smile on her face as she found the perfect spot for it among the branches.

"I wonder who this Sam person was," she mused, gently placing the ornament back into its wrapping. "Nana never mentioned him to me."

He shrugged, a hint of a smile playing at the corners of his mouth. "There's a lot about your grandmother's life that I think we're both discovering. She had a way of keeping certain things close to her heart."

"I wonder if we could find out who he was and why Nana had the ornament."

"We could do some digging. See if we can find out anything about a glass blower who might have lived on the island. Let me grab my laptop." He returned with it and opened it, his fingers grazing the keys as he typed on the keyboard.

She leaned over his shoulder, watching the words appear on the screen. "Look." She pointed. "A Sam Waterman used to have a glass-blowing company. Click on that link."

He clicked on it and a large article came up about the man. "It says he had the business back in the 1920s. Almost lost it during the Great Depression. But someone in town showed his ornaments to a buyer at Macy's department store. Macy's placed a large order and his business was saved."

"I wonder who did that?"

"I don't know, but I'm not surprised. People on Belle Island take care of one another."

"So we know who made this and why it's

important to Belle Island history. You think that's why she had it?"

"Probably. Miss G did like to learn about the local history."

He nodded toward the box. "Want to see what else is in here?"

"You know, I think I'd rather wait until tomorrow. Open one each day. One at a time."

"Oh, kind of like Miss G's advent calendar. She gave me one. I loved it. She refilled it every year."

"She gave you one too? She gave me one when I was a little girl." Her heart warmed at the memory. "And each Christmas I couldn't wait to get here for the holidays and open one drawer a day. She'd put in little charms, or a special seashell, or a piece of candy. Every day was a new surprise."

He tilted his head, watching her closely. "So, we'll do that with this box? Open one each day?"

"Absolutely. What a great idea. I bet Nana would approve."

"I have the feeling she would, too." He nodded his head slowly and smiled.

She returned his smile. Randy seemed to

understand her in ways that no one except Nana ever had.

CHAPTER 7

Evie turned from pouring a cup of coffee when a knock sounded at the door. She glanced at the clock, noting it was early, but probably not too early for visitors. She opened the door to find Randy standing there, a box from The Sweet Shoppe in his hands.

"Morning. I hope I'm not interrupting anything," he said, a sheepish grin on his face. "I brought cinnamon rolls from The Sweet Shoppe. Thought we could have breakfast together before we take a look at the next item in the box."

She smiled. "That sounds perfect. Come on in. I'm anxious to open another item too."

He stepped inside and looked around the

cottage. "No Christmas decorations? Can't remember a December without this cottage crammed with holiday decorations."

"No. I don't think I'm going to put anything up this year. It's just too… hard."

He looked at her with understanding. "I guess it would be hard." He shrugged. "Or maybe it might cheer you up."

Maybe. But she didn't think so

He followed her into the kitchen where she poured him a cup of coffee, and then they settled at the kitchen table, the aroma of freshly brewed coffee mingling with the sweet scent of the cinnamon rolls. As they ate, they chatted about their plans for the day. "I really am going to do some more sorting through Nana's things. I can't avoid it forever."

"Sometimes the hard jobs are better when they're faced head-on and we just work our way through them."

"Yes, you're right. I'm going to make sure I make some headway each day. Then, eventually, it will all be over." If she could ever make decisions on what to keep and what to give away. It felt like everything held so many precious memories.

After they finished their breakfast, she cleared the table and retrieved the box from the living room. She set it on the table between them, and they both looked at it with anticipation.

"Ready to see what's next?" she asked, her fingers hovering over the lid.

He nodded, leaning forward in his chair.

She carefully lifted the lid and reached inside. The item she pulled out was slim, flat, and rectangular. Gently, she unwrapped the tissue paper to reveal one old index card on top and an even older, yellowed one beneath it.

She looked at the first card. "It's a recipe," she said, turning the card over in her hands. "For sugar cookies."

He leaned closer, studying the handwritten script. "It looks like Miss G's handwriting."

She ran her finger over the faded ink, a lump forming in her throat. "I remember these cookies. Nana used to make them every Christmas. We'd decorate them together, and she'd let me sneak bites of the dough when she thought no one was looking."

"That sounds like Miss G. Always ready with a treat and a bit of mischief."

"Nana knew the recipe by heart, so I've never even seen this card." She picked up the other card and frowned. "Look, it's the same recipe, but in a different handwriting. And it says Herbert's on it."

"I wonder who Herbert was?" Randy frowned.

She laughed. "I'll get my laptop and see if we have as much luck as we did last night."

She grabbed her laptop, and they searched for Herbert and Belle Island. Quite a few entries came up. Randy pointed to one. "Look, there was a Herbert's Bakery back in the 1930s. You think this recipe could be from his bakery?"

She typed in Herbert's Bakery and a half dozen entries came up. One was a photo of an old newspaper article. She enlarged the photo, and they squinted, trying to make out the words.

"It says Herbert donated twelve dozen sugar cookies to the Christmas Festival. They were raising money for the school."

"So, all these years, my Nana was keeping the tradition when she would bake that same recipe and donate the cookies to the Christmas Festival?"

"Looks like it." Randy nodded.

"There is just so much I didn't know about

her. But I do remember making these each Christmas. We'd package them up and deliver them to the festival."

"Why don't we make them?" Randy's eyes lit up with the idea. "We could honor your grandmother's memory by baking a batch of her famous sugar cookies."

She hesitated. "I… I don't know. It wouldn't be the same without her."

He reached across the table and placed his hand over hers. "I understand. But maybe it's a way to feel closer to her, to keep her traditions alive. We could even make enough to donate to the festival, just like Miss G did. The festival is this coming weekend."

She looked down at the recipe card, the familiar loops and swirls of her grandmother's handwriting blurring as tears filled her eyes. Randy was right. Baking the cookies would be a way to honor Nana, to keep a piece of her alive in the present. And to give back to the community, just like Nana had.

"Okay," she said, her voice thick with emotion. "Let's do it. Let's bake Nana's—or I guess they are really Herbert's—sugar cookies."

Randy squeezed her hand. "I'll help you.

We can make a day of it, just like you used to with Miss G."

"Now that sounds like a wonderful idea. I'd love the help."

Randy stepped into the familiar kitchen, memories of countless baking sessions with Genevieve washing over him. The layout hadn't changed much over the years, and he could almost picture Miss G bustling about, gathering ingredients and humming holiday tunes.

He smiled as Evie gathered bowls and utensils and enthusiastically got on board with the idea of baking the cookies. For the first time since he met her, there was no hint of sadness haunting her eyes.

"You know, I sat there at the kitchen table watching Miss G bake so many times. We'd chat as she puttered in her kitchen. She taught me to bake, too. Though I never was as good a baker as she was." He reached into the cupboard and pulled out the flour and sugar. "I swear I know where everything is in this kitchen from my hours spent here."

He offered to measure out the dry

ingredients as she got out the other ingredients from the fridge. Working side by side with Evie, he found himself relaxing into the comfortable rhythm of baking. He paused as he sifted the flour. "You know, the first time I tried to make these, I accidentally used salt instead of sugar. Miss G never let me live that one down."

Evie's laughter rang out across the kitchen. "I can just imagine Nana's face when she tasted those cookies."

"Oh, she had quite the reaction," He grinned and shook his head at the memory. "But she was patient, helping me start a new batch and teaching me the importance of double-checking ingredients."

As they continued mixing the dough and Evie added the salt, their hands accidentally brushed. A spark of connection spread through him. He quickly recovered and quipped, "Make sure you use the correct amount for salt and not the amount for sugar."

"Right. Don't want to repeat your mistakes," she teased back.

As he rolled out the dough, Randy began to recount memories of past Christmases on the island. "The holiday cookie fundraiser used to be quite the event. People would gather at the community center, each bringing their own special recipe to share. The tables would be overflowing with every type of cookie imaginable. People were always so generous with their donations of baked goods."

"I remember it from when I was a young girl. And there was always the gingerbread house decorating competition." Her eyes lit up at the memories.

"I won that one year," he bragged.

"You did?" She looked at him with an expression that clearly said she was doubtful.

"Miss G convinced me to enter. I made a gingerbread house that looked like Magic Cafe. I mean, really, who wouldn't vote for a Magic Cafe gingerbread house?"

She laughed again. "You're right about that. Magic Cafe would always be the clear winner."

He was enjoying making her laugh, watching her eyes light up, seeing her smile. "And there was always Christmas music and then the tree lighting that evening."

"Oh, the tree lighting. I loved that."

"So you want to go to the festival and the tree lighting with me this Saturday?" He looked at her, hoping she'd say yes.

Her eyes lit up with excitement. "I'd love to.

I came here thinking I would avoid all things Christmas since it's my first one without Nana… but now I find I'm getting into the holiday spirit."

"I'm glad." Happiness surged through him. Miss G would be pleased with him, making sure Evie enjoyed the holidays.

She reached out and touched his arm, and that same connection ricocheted through him. "You're the reason I'm enjoying it. Thanks for pulling me out of my mood and making me realize Nana wouldn't want me to mope around."

He covered her hand with his own. "Glad to help. Now let's get out those cookie cutters and get started."

Evie picked up the star. "Oh, Nana loved this simple star shape. And she'd decorate it so pretty."

"She did." He picked up the reindeer one. "This is my favorite, but I swear the antlers are always breaking off."

She laughed. "Happened to mine too. Oh look, the Santa one, and the angel. I think I love all of them."

"Then we'll have to make all of them." He paused, then decided to plunge on. "And we need some Christmas music. Doesn't seem right to make Christmas cookies without Christmas music."

She paused a moment, then nodded. "You're right. Nana always had it playing while she baked the cookies."

She left the kitchen, and he glanced out into the living room and saw her pick out a Christmas album and put it on the turntable. No digital music for Miss G. Only her beloved albums. Soon the mellow voice of Perry Como drifted through the cottage.

Evie came back into the kitchen, smiling. "I love this album. I'd play it over and over, but Nana wouldn't ever complain."

"It's a great choice."

He pulled out the well-worn baking sheets from the cupboard, and with them came memories of countless batches of cookies made with Miss G. He glanced over at Evie, her brow creased in concentration as she meticulously cut out star from the dough before moving on to tree shapes.

They worked in comfortable silence. The only sounds were the gentle thud of the cookie cutters and the soft Christmas music playing in the background.

He found himself sneaking glances at Evie, admiring the way her hair fell softly around her face and the determined set of her jaw as she focused on making each cookie perfect.

As they loaded up the baking sheets, the kitchen filled with the warm, inviting scent of baking cookies. "I think Nana would be proud of us," Evie said softly, sliding the last tray into the oven. "Carrying on her tradition like this."

He nodded, his throat unexpectedly tightening with emotion. "She'd be thrilled to see you here in her kitchen, baking her recipes."

Evie's eyes glistened with unshed tears, but she smiled. "Thank you for doing this with me. It means more than you know."

He reached out and gently squeezed her hand. "I'm glad to be here with you."

As the timer dinged, they pulled the last batch of golden, perfectly shaped cookies from the oven, the scent of vanilla and spices wafting through the air. As he helped Evie transfer them to cooling racks, their hands brushing occasionally and sent little sparks of electricity through him.

Sparks he tried to ignore. But he had to admit he was helpless against them.

Once the cookies had cooled, Evie went to

the pantry and pulled out a collection of tins, each one a different size and shape. Randy recognized them immediately—Miss G's cookie tins—the ones she'd use every year to package her famous Christmas cookies for the festival. She was always picking up new ones to add to her collection to replenish it. Miss G always said that cookies were meant to be given away in cookie tins, like it was some kind of universal rule.

"She kept them," Evie murmured, running her fingers along the edges of a particularly intricate tin. "I remember helping her fill these when I was a little girl."

He nodded as the fleeting vision of a young Evie, her pigtails bobbing as she carefully arranged cookies, flashed through his mind. "She cherished those moments with you, you know."

Together, they began filling the tins, layering the cookies in festive tissue paper. Soon each tin was filled and sealed. A feeling of accomplishment swept through him at being a part of honoring Miss G's memory in a way that would have made her proud.

He stepped back to admire their handiwork.

The tins were stacked neatly on the counter, ready to be delivered to the festival.

"We did it," Evie said softly. "I swear I can actually feel her here with us in the kitchen."

"I know." He draped his arm around her shoulders and tucked her up against him. "I can too."

CHAPTER 8

The next morning Evie made her way over to Randy's house, Christmas box clutched in her hands. As he opened the door, she grinned at him. "I just couldn't open the next item alone. I feel like this is something we're doing together." She didn't voice the thought lingering in her mind—or fully acknowledge it to herself—that she'd simply wanted to see him. After baking the cookies with him yesterday, she felt a closeness to him and found herself looking forward to sharing the ritual of opening a new item with him.

His face lit up with a wide grin. "I'm good with that. Come on in." He held the door open, and she slipped inside. "I just brewed some coffee. Would you like a cup?"

"Yes, that would be lovely, thank you."

He disappeared into the kitchen and returned moments later with two steaming mugs of coffee. They settled onto his comfortable couch, the Christmas box between them. She motioned toward it. "It's your turn to choose this time."

"Are you sure?"

"Absolutely, I insist."

Randy leaned forward and reached in. His hand hovered over one item before moving to another. He carefully lifted out a small package, then seemed to reconsider and selected a different one.

"Unwrap it. Let's see what it is." She nodded encouragingly.

He peeled away the tissue paper, revealing a well-worn Christmas stocking. "Well, would you look at that," he said softly, holding it up for her to see. "It appears to be hand knit." He smiled slightly. "I'm kind of an expert on what hand-knit items look like. Miss G always had her knitting with her."

"She did." She leaned in for a closer look. "And it does look hand knit. I wonder whose it was?" She reached for it and turned it over in her hands. "It doesn't have a name on it or even initials. I guess this is one that we'll never figure out."

As she ran her fingers along the soft, aged fabric, she noticed something peculiar about the toe. Frowning, she carefully slipped her hand inside the stocking. To her surprise, her fingers brushed against something tucked away in its depths. Slowly, she withdrew an old photograph, its edges slightly curled and faded with time.

"Here, take a look at this." She handed the photograph to Randy.

He accepted it, his eyes narrowing as he studied the image. "It's a young man in uniform." He turned the photo over, running his fingers along the blank surface. "No name or date on the back, though."

She sighed. "I suppose that's it then. An item with a mystery we'll never unravel."

His eyes lit up. "Let's not throw in the towel just yet. We could pay a visit to the historical society. Etta might be able to help us piece together this puzzle."

"From just the photo?" She looked at him doubtfully.

"Maybe. It's at least worth a shot."

"I'm game. Let's see if she can help us."

They took his truck over to the historical

society, where a woman was just opening the door. "Good morning, Randy."

"Etta, this is Evie. She's Miss Genevieve's granddaughter."

Etta turned to her. "Oh, I heard you were here on the island. I'm so sorry for your loss. Miss Genevieve was a wonderful woman. She loved looking into the history of the island. We had many a long chat."

"Thank you." Evie waited for the tears to creep into her eyes, but thankfully, this time, no tears. "And her love of the history of the island. That's kind of why we're here. I found this wooden box in the storage room at Nana's. And she had all these items in it carefully wrapped up. We found an ornament handmade by a glass blower that used to have a shop on the island."

"Oh, yes. Sam Waterman. I've read about him. He had some troubles during the Great Depression. An anonymous benefactor from the island showed his work to a buyer from a large department store. They made a large order and his shop was saved."

"Exactly. And we found an original handwritten sugar cookie recipe from a bakery on the island. Herbert's."

"I recall reading about that bakery, too."

"And Nana used that recipe for her sugar cookies each Christmas."

"No kidding. She didn't tell me that." Etta smiled. "But they sure were delicious."

She held up the stocking and the photo. "Now we found this. An old stocking. And we found a photo inside it."

"Well, come inside, and let's see if we can figure out where the stocking came from." Etta motioned them inside.

They sat at a large wooden table, and she handed the photo to Etta. The woman looked at it carefully. "Looks like a World War II uniform."

"But how would we ever figure out who he was?"

"I have a file somewhere. It's in the old paper files that haven't been scanned yet. That scanning is quite the project. I have to coax our old computers to take the uploads of the scans. Give me a minute or so and let me see if I can find it."

Etta disappeared, and Evie turned to Randy. "You think she'll be able to help us?"

"If anyone can, she can."

Etta returned with a stack of files in her hands. She sat down and opened the top file.

"Ah, ha. I knew we had this. A list of islanders who fought in World War II. Looks like we had a dozen men who fought."

"But how do we figure out if this stocking was one of theirs?"

Etta picked up another file. "There are photos from that time period in here. Let's see what we find." She set the photos out, one by one. But none held any clue.

Frustration swept through her. Maybe they really wouldn't figure out why this stocking was in Nana's box.

"Wait, this might help." Etta held out a photo of eight men in uniform. She flipped it over and smiled. "And some kind soul wrote the names of the men on the back."

They all looked closely at the photo. "That man at the end..." Evie pointed. "Does that look like the same man in our photo?"

"It does, kind of. It's so faded though." Randy frowned. "What is his name?" He pointed to the last man in the photo.

Etta flipped it over. "That's Warren Guthrie. That will help us. Let's see what we can find out about Warren. We've got photos of the high school graduating class from every year. That's already scanned and online." She scooted over to the computer and typed into the search bar. The computer just sat there. "Come on, girl. You can do it," Etta said encouragingly to the machine. As if it heard her, it popped up a grid of photos.

"There—that's him, right?" She pointed to a young man.

"Sure looks like him." Randy nodded.

Etta typed into the computer again and read the screen. She clicked and read some more. "Listen to this. It looks like Warren's mother passed away and that was all the family he had. It says the town all got together and sent items to him in 1943. There's a list of items. Razors, bars of homemade soap, candy, and look here. A hand-knit Christmas stocking."

"You think this is that stocking?" She peered at the article on the screen.

"I'd have to think so." Etta nodded as she clicked the mouse again and another photo popped up.

"Look… it's there." Evie clapped her hands in excitement. "On that table with all the gifts."

Randy leaned in, reading the words under the article. "It says the Christmas stocking was knit by Mrs. Chancey."

Her mouth dropped open in surprise. "That

would have been some relative of Nana's, right? Well, a relative of Grandfather's, I suppose."

"Right, because Miss G married into the Chancey family." Randy nodded.

"So you think that's how Nana ended up with it?"

"Maybe." Randy smiled. "Maybe she heard this story and found the stocking and saved it. Part of her history."

Suddenly, a terrible thought struck her. She swallowed hard. "Etta… do you know if Warren made it back from the war?" she asked softly.

"Let's see if we can find mention of him after 1945." Etta clicked way on the keyboard, searching. Soon her face broke into a wide smile. "Look here. It's Warren and his wife and two little girls."

Relief rushed through her. "Oh, I'm so glad."

"Looks like we have a happy ending to this item." Randy grinned.

Her smile widened as she met his gaze, a warm feeling of success and happiness washing over her. Their mission to uncover the stories behind Nana's Christmas box treasures was proving more successful than she'd dared hope. And she realized part of her happiness was from how much she enjoyed sharing this journey with Randy. His enthusiasm matched her own, making the research feel less like a task and more like an adventure.

"I never imagined we'd find out so much about these old keepsakes. It's like piecing together a family puzzle."

Randy nodded, his expression mirroring her satisfaction. "Your grandmother would be proud," he said, his voice gentle. "We're honoring her memory by bringing these stories to light."

CHAPTER 9

Randy held the door open for Evie as they left the historical society. Evie was lost in thought, her expression pensive.

"That was quite the story about the town sending Warren the Christmas package after his mom died, wasn't it?"

"It was. And I'm so glad he made it back from the war. He looked very happy in that photo with his family."

"So far we've had good luck figuring out the story behind each item, haven't we?"

"We have." She nodded.

"You know, with all these memories we're discovering, maybe you'd want to decorate the cottage for the holidays. It could be a nice way to honor your grandmother and the traditions she kept alive. Would you like that?"

Evie hesitated, a flicker of uncertainty in her eyes. "I… I don't know. I was kind of going to ignore the whole Christmas thing this year." She laughed softly. "But that sure isn't working out like I planned, is it? What with the Christmas box and baking Christmas cookies."

He grinned at her. "No, not exactly like you planned."

They locked gazes, and for a moment he was afraid she would reject the idea.

"You know what? Yes. Let's decorate the cottage. Nana would love that." She frowned. "But I don't have a tree. Nana would have nothing to do with an artificial tree. Always a real one."

"Then let's head to the Christmas tree lot and get you a tree."

A smile tugged at the corners of her mouth. "Okay, let's do it."

Proud of himself that he'd convinced her to decorate, he took her arm and led her to the truck. Truth be told, he just couldn't image Miss G's cottage without holiday decorations.

He opened the truck door for her, and she climbed inside. They made their way to the local Christmas tree lot, just down the street from The Sweet Shoppe. The scent of pine and the twinkle of Christmas lights greeted them as they entered. Evie's eyes lit up, the holiday spirit seeming to wash over her as she took in the rows of beautiful trees.

Christmas music drifted over the lot as Evie carefully looked at tree after tree. "It has to be a balsam fir. Nana says that's the best tree and is the most aromatic."

As they continued looking, he wondered if she would ever make up her mind. But the concentration on her features as she carefully inspected each tree amused him. It was so like Miss G when he'd taken her to pick up her tree. Must run in the family.

Finally, she came to a stop in front of a stunning balsam fir, its branches full and even, the perfect shape for decorating. She circled the tree, taking in its beauty from every angle. Then she turned to him and threw out her arm. "Ta-da. This is it. It's perfect. Just like the ones Nana would pick out."

"This one it is, then." His heart warmed seeing the look of joy on her face.

They paid for the tree, and he placed it in the back of this truck for the drive back to her cottage. Once inside, Evie pointed. “It goes right by the window over there.”

He laughed. “I’m well aware of where it goes. I’ve set up Miss G’s tree for her ever since I moved next door.”

She turned to him, surprise in her eyes. “You did? I didn’t know that.”

“Yep. And helped her decorate it. She always repaid me by inviting me for a nice dinner and sending me home with leftovers and a plate of cookies. I always told her I got the better end of the arrangement.” He grinned.

“I’m glad you were here to help her with things like that.” She frowned. “I should have made time to come back here more. Nana never complained and traveled to see me. Said she knew I was busy. But… still… I wish I would have made more of an effort to come here.”

“I’m sure Miss G understood.”

“I’m sure she did. But it didn’t make it right.” She shrugged. “But she always said we end up where we’re supposed to be. I guess I was meant to live in the city.”

“Well, she’d be glad that you’re decorating the cottage now. Miss G did love the holidays.”

“She would be glad, wouldn’t she?” Evie’s lips curled up in a gentle smile. “Let’s get the stand for the tree and get it set up. Then we can haul out the decorations."

Soon they had the tree in the stand and Evie commanded him to turn it this way and that, move it to the right, to the left. He smiled to himself. It was just like putting up the tree for Miss G.

After the tree was exactly like Evie wanted it, they strung the lights on it. She disappeared into the storage room and returned with a box of Christmas ornaments.

Her excitement as she remembered so many of the ornaments tickled him. Each one brought a wide smile to her face. The Rudolph ornament she'd made for her grandmother when she was a little girl. A replica of the lighthouse here on Belle Island. A small silver ornament frame with a photo of Evie and Miss G. One by one, they hung them on the tree.

Finally, it was time for the tree topper. She got out the stepstool and climbed up on it. He handed her the star, keeping a hand on her back to make sure she didn't fall. Once it was secure atop the tree, she climbed down and stood back, hands on hips, very much a carbon copy of her grandmother. "Okay, now we need to plug in the lights."

He did as requested and watched while Evie stood, mesmerized by the tree.

"It's... so beautiful. Just like how I remembered it." The emotion was evident in her voice as she choked on the words.

"Miss G would be so happy to see this," he said softly, knowing he was telling the truth.

She turned to him, her eyes glistening with wonder. "Thank you for helping me with this."

"My pleasure." And he meant it. He was fairly certain he'd enjoyed it as much as, if not more than, Evie.

"I should probably let you go. I've monopolized your whole day," she said.

"Not before we get out the caroling mice." He looked at her in mock horror. "Those have to be set up."

She laughed out loud. "Nana always insisted they be put in a different spot each year."

"Then I'll be sure to tell you if you're repeating a spot she put them out in over the last few years."

They found a place for the mice on the bookshelf, standing on a copy of "A Christmas Carol" for a special touch of festivity. He assured her she'd found an original spot. Then she set out the Christmas angel and wound it up so they could watch it spin slowly in circles as the sound of "Silent Night" drifted through the room.

She turned to him. "This has been the best day that I've had in a very long time."

"You know what? Me too." And he realized it was the best day he'd had in as long as he could remember. Evie was so easy to be with, and he loved seeing her eyes light up with treasured memories.

She grinned. "Now, I need to keep up Nana's side of the bargain. Only I don't have anything here to cook. How about I take you out to eat? Looks like we've worked right through lunch. You must be starving."

"I wouldn't say no to lunch." And it would mean he could spend more time with her. Startled, he realized it was something he wanted more and more with each passing day.

"I could take you to The Sweet Shoppe," Evie suggested. She'd loved the loaf of bread she'd gotten from them at the open-air market and the cinnamon rolls Randy had brought. And she'd heard they had sandwiches at lunchtime.

Randy looked at his watch. "Ah, a bit too late. Julie closes at two in the afternoon."

Oh, bummer. She scrunched up her face and thought for a moment. "Magic Cafe?"

"I never say no to Magic Cafe." He grinned.

"I could go for a fried grouper sandwich. And hush puppies. I love Tally's hush puppies."

"Me too. Sounds like we're ordering the same thing. Want to walk or drive?"

"Let's walk if that's okay with you. I love being able to walk to so many places here on the island."

It was a short walk to Magic Cafe, and Tally greeted them with a smile. "Late lunch for you two today?"

"Randy was helping me decorate for Christmas."

"Ah, good. Can't have a bare cottage this time of year, now can we? Genevieve did love her holidays. Come, I'll get you a table near the beach, just like you both like it."

She turned to Randy. "You get a table at the edge near the beach? I know some people don't like it because it's a bit sandy under the tables there."

"My favorite spot," he assured her.

They both ordered and Tally brought them

large glasses of sweet tea. Evie took a sip, savoring the flavor. "They don't know how to make sweet tea up north. They just dump some sugar in iced tea and call it good." She shook her head. "I do love coming down here and getting real sweet tea."

"Sounds like you're liking a lot of things down here. Walking to places. The tea. Decorating the cottage."

"I am enjoying myself." She paused, frowning. "I thought it would be terrible coming here. All the memories of Nana. And it was hard at first, and sometimes I expect to turn around and see her coming out of her kitchen." She shrugged. "But, as the days go by, I find that it's… it's more comforting in a way. More than I expected."

"I'm glad."

She grinned at him. "And some guy talked me into decorating and actually enjoying the Christmas season. Who knew?"

He laughed. "Right, who knew?"

She looked out at the gulf as contentment spread through her. The rhythm of the waves as they rolled to shore was so comforting. It felt so right to be here. At least for the holidays. She'd stay here that long, she promised herself.

Just then, Tally returned with their orders, the tantalizing aroma of fried seafood wafting through the air.

"Here we are," Tally announced cheerfully, placing two plates before them.

Evie's mouth watered as she took in the sight of the fried grouper sandwiches. The golden-brown fillet, crispy and perfectly breaded, peeked out from between the soft, toasted bun. She took a bite, closing her eyes to better savor it. The grouper was tender and juicy, a perfect contrast to the crunch of the breading. She chased it with a hush puppy. Tally's hush puppies had a slight tang to them, with deliciously crunchy outsides and rich, sweet corn inside, the perfect complement to her sandwich.

She looked over at Randy as she wiped her napkin over her mouth. "These are as wonderful as I remembered."

"Can't beat 'em anywhere. That's for sure," he agreed as he popped one into his mouth.

As she reached for her glass of tea, a thought struck her. "You know," she began softly, "I hadn't realized how much I missed this place, this way of life. It's like… like I lost part of myself when I was away."

He took a sip of his tea, his eyes thoughtful.

"Sometimes, you need to come back to where you felt you belonged to remember who you are."

"I think you might be right." Because this was the most content she'd felt in a long time. And instead of the pain of missing Nana stabbing her every waking moment, she felt close to her grandmother here. Almost as if she were right here with her.

CHAPTER 10

Evie had just finished making a pot of coffee when she heard a knock at the door. Smiling as she went to answer it, she was certain she'd find Randy standing there.

And he was, with a warm smile and a paper bag in his hand.

"Good morning," he greeted her cheerfully. "I know you said to come over this morning and we'd open another item from the Christmas box. I brought some fresh peach scones from The Sweet Shoppe. Thought we could have breakfast together out on the porch."

The aroma of freshly baked scones wafting from the bag made her stomach rumble. She laughed as she opened the door wider.

"Breakfast together is getting to be quite the habit."

As Randy stepped inside, she noticed how at ease he seemed in her grandmother's cottage. It struck her how much of a fixture he must have been in Nana's life.

"The porch sounds lovely," she said, heading to the kitchen to grab mugs and plates. "Let me just get these, and we can head out there."

Balancing the mugs and plates, she led the way to the porch and set the items on the table. The morning air was a bit chilly, so she went back in and grabbed her Nana's favorite wrap. Settling it around her shoulders, she headed back outside, pausing a moment to take in the view. It never disappointed.

"This is perfect," she said, settling into one of the chairs. "It's so peaceful out here in the mornings."

"It is peaceful. Miss G and I would often have coffee out here." Randy placed the bag on the table and began unpacking the scones. "And they're still warm."

As he handed her a scone, their fingers brushed briefly, and a little flutter started in her chest. She pushed the feeling aside, focusing instead on the delicious treat in her hand.

"So," Randy said, relaxing into the chair beside her, "ready to unwrap another item from the box?"

She nodded, taking a sip of her coffee. "I am. It's been surprisingly therapeutic, going through these items. Like I'm getting to know a different side of Nana."

"She was a remarkable woman," he agreed. "Always full of stories about the island and its people."

As they enjoyed their breakfast, she found herself relaxing into an easy conversation with Randy. The gentle clink of coffee mugs and the soft sound of the waves provided a soothing backdrop to their chat. It felt natural, sitting here on the porch, sharing stories and laughter. The cottage was beginning to feel more like home to her.

But it wasn't home, she reminded herself. She had a place back up north. And she really needed to get back there and find another job.

Her fingers tightened around her mug as she considered the reality of her situation. Not many high-tech jobs here on Belle Island, so it was silly to think she could live here. She glanced around at the lush greenery and listened to the sound of waves, feeling an unexpected tug of longing.

Live here? Permanently? Where had that thought come from? She blinked, surprised by the direction of her thoughts. But it was a silly notion anyway. She pushed it away, focusing instead on the last of her delicious scone.

As they finished their meal and sat sipping their coffee, the conversation lulled into a comfortable silence. She found herself stealing glances at Randy, wondering what he was thinking. He leaned back in his chair, looking completely at ease.

Finally, she set her mug down with a soft clink. "I guess it's time. Let me go get the box." She stood and stretched slightly before heading inside. When she returned, she set the box on the table between them, her fingers lingering on its worn edges for a moment before she pulled away.

"Go ahead. Pick one." He nodded toward the box.

She stared into the box, her fingers hovering over the various wrapped items as she debated which one to choose. Why did it seem like such a big decision? She finally made up her mind and took one out. She gently untied the twine and unwrapped the tissue paper to reveal a small, carved box. As she opened the lid, a tinkling, melodic waltz filled the air.

She listened, entranced, as the delicate melody of "The Skater's Waltz" filled the air. The familiar tune brought back memories of Nana playing it on her old stereo, the music floating through the cottage on lazy summer afternoons.

When the tune stopped, she passed the music box to Randy, watching as he examined it closely. His eyes lit up as he turned it over. "Look, it's engraved. To Lula, all my love. Fred. 3/2/1908."

"Oh." She leaned closer to see. "1908? It's over a century old. I wonder who Lula and Fred were."

He pulled out his phone. "Let's see what we can find online." But despite his efforts, searching for Lula and Fred on the island yielded no results. Even the date didn't bring up any significant events.

"I'm not sure we can solve this one," he said as he set his phone down.

She let out a sigh. "We were on a winning streak, but it's unrealistic to think we'd find out the significance of all these items."

"Maybe, but even if we don't know all the details, it's clear Miss G saw something special in each of these items. That's what really matters, isn't it?"

"Yes, you're right. That's what matters." She was still disappointed they couldn't figure out the story behind the music box though.

Randy handed the box back to her. "You know, hearing the music, it reminded me. There's the Christmas dance tonight at the town center. It's our official kickoff for the Christmas Festival. Would you like to go?"

"Oh, that sounds like fun."

"It's kind of a chance for everyone to dress up fancy for a change."

"Oh, I didn't bring anything nice to wear."

"I'm sure anything you wear will be fine."

Spoken like a true male. Maybe she'd have time to go shopping. At this rate, she was never going to get Nana's cottage sorted out.

Randy stood. "I should go get some work done. I'll pick you up about seven?"

"Sure. And thanks for bringing breakfast. The scones were delicious."

"Thanks for sharing the opening of another piece from the Christmas box." With a quick wave, he clambered down the porch steps and jogged over to his cottage.

She picked up their dishes and carried them inside, then brought the Christmas box in. Maybe she should head into town to try to find a dress to wear.

She sighed, knowing she was procrastinating on what she needed to be doing. She really, *really* needed to do something—anything—toward sorting out the cottage first.

She'd been avoiding Nana's room, but she couldn't avoid it forever. Now seemed like the time. Squaring her shoulders, she headed into Nana's bedroom. The closet. She'd start there.

She stepped into the closet as sunlight from the far window partially illuminated the space. She flipped the switch, and soft light filled the rest of the area.

With a deep breath, she began sorting through the clothes, carefully folding tops and slacks into a box. "Someone will appreciate these," she said out loud to no one, imagining Nana's approving smile at the thought of her clothes finding new homes.

As she worked, her eye caught on something tucked away in the corner. She moved some clothing to reveal a package underneath.

Curious, she reached for it. Her breath caught as she read the gift tag. "To Evie," it said in Nana's elegant script, followed by a short message: "When I saw this, I just knew you had to have it. Merry Christmas, Nana."

With trembling fingers, she unwrapped the gift. Silky fabric spilled out from the festive green wrapping paper revealing a stunning red dress. She held it up, the fabric soft against her skin, and felt a lump form in her throat. It was perfect for the Christmas dance. Almost as if Nana had known she would need it. She hugged the dress close, feeling a connection to her grandmother that transcended time and space.

Randy stood at Evie's front door, adjusting his tie yet again. He realized he hadn't felt this nervous—or hopeful—in years. The air was thick with possibility and the scent of saltwater as he smoothed his tie one last time.

Why was he so nervous? He was simply taking Evie to the Christmas dance. That was all.

And yet, when he knocked on the door, his breath caught in his throat as he waited for her to appear, and he had to wonder if she could hear his heart pounding from inside the house.

The door swung open and his neatly planned world tilted on its axis. Evie stood framed in the doorway, a vision that stole his breath away. A soft red dress hugged her curves and shimmered softly in the porch light. Her dark hair was swept up, exposing the elegant curve of her neck. A few loose tendrils framed her face. Her eyes seemed to sparkle with an inner light, reflecting the Christmas lights strung along the porch.

He swallowed. Hard. "Wow, if that's what you call not bringing anything nice to wear..."

Her lips curved into a gentle smile that made his heart skip a beat. "It's a Christmas present from Nana. I guess she bought it early but never had— She didn't get a chance to give it to me. I found it when I was cleaning out her closet. It's a beautiful dress, isn't it?"

He opened his mouth to speak, to tell her how great she looked, but the words caught in his throat. All he could do was stand there, drinking in the sight of her, feeling like the luckiest man on the island.

He finally pulled himself together. "It's

beautiful. *You're* beautiful." The words just came out before he had a chance to stop them.

An adorable blush swept across her cheeks. "Ah… thank you. You look good too. Handsome, I mean."

He was glad he'd decided to wear the one suit he owned instead of his sports coat. After adjusting his tie yet again, he held out his arm. "Ready?"

She nodded and pulled the door shut behind her. She took his arm, and a spark of electricity jolted through him. Trying to ignore it, he helped her into the passenger seat, struggling not to let his nervousness show.

As he drove, she exclaimed excitedly about the various decorations around the town. The white lights adorning Belle Island Inn. The wreaths on the lampposts. The twinkle lights at the gazebo.

"The town looks like it should be on a Christmas postcard. It's so festive and pretty."

"Belle Island does like its Christmas season, I admit."

He parked the car, and they got out. A sense of pride swept through him when she took his arm. He undoubtedly had the most beautiful woman at the dance by his side—not to mention she was smart and easy to talk to. He wasn't sure how he'd gotten so lucky.

"Look, there's Tally. Let's go say hi," Evie said as they entered the dance.

He led her over to where Tally was standing, looking festive in a dark green dress with a pretty Christmas pin on it.

"Evie, dear. You look lovely." Tally hugged her. "Glad you could come to our Christmas dance."

"Thank you," Evie beamed. "Nana got it for me."

"Well, it certainly suits you." Tally turned and waved, and Julie came up to them. "Julie, have you met Evie? Genevieve's granddaughter."

Julie held out her hand, and Evie shook it. "No, I haven't. Nice to meet you."

"Nice to meet you. I've been enjoying having breakfast from your shop. We had the peach scones today. They were delicious."

Julie smiled at the compliment. "I'm glad you enjoyed them. Always a customer favorite."

Tally turned and looked at him expectantly. "Aren't you going to ask Evie to dance? Shame not to show off that beautiful dress."

He flashed a grin. "Yes, ma'am. I was just

going to ask her. Evie? Would you care to dance?"

"I'd love to."

She smiled up at him, and his heart thumped wildly.

Get a grip, buddy.

She slipped her hand in his as he led her out onto the dance floor. The cheerful Christmas song ended and a slow song started. He gently placed his hand on her waist, acutely aware of their closeness as they began to sway to the music.

She leaned her head against his chest and he almost forgot how to dance. Recovering, he held her against him, certain she could now hear his heart pounding against her cheek.

As the song faded away, Evie stepped back from his embrace and a sudden void swept over him. Her eyes sparkled as she looked up at him, her smile warm and genuine. "That was nice," she said softly.

His heart raced, making it difficult to form coherent thoughts. "It… was," he managed to say, his voice sounding strained even to his own ears. He cleared his throat, hoping to regain some composure. "Um, would you like some punch?"

The words tumbled out, and he inwardly cringed. Was he coming across as awkward and inexperienced? He hadn't felt this nervous around a woman in years, and it threw him off balance.

"Yes, thank you."

He made his way through the crowd to the refreshment table, his gaze continually drawn back to Evie. As she chatted animatedly with Julie, he marveled at how effortlessly she seemed to blend in with the island's residents. There was something about her warmth and genuine interest that drew people in, making it look like she'd always been a part of their community.

With two glasses of punch in hand, he returned to the two women. "Here you go, Evie," he said, handing her a glass. Then he turned to Julie, extending the other. "Julie, would you like this?"

Julie shook her head with a smile. "No, but thank you. I'm off to find Susan." She gave them both a quick wave before disappearing into the crowd.

Randy turned to Evie as he took a sip of the punch. "Susan owns Belle Island Inn. You'll have to meet her, too. She runs the inn with her son." He found himself wanting to explain all the things about the island, the people, the places, in the hope that Evie would feel at home here.

And maybe even… stay here on the island.

There—he'd allowed himself to actually think the thought. But it was a silly one. She was here to clear out Miss G's things. He hoped she at least stayed through the holidays though. And New Year's. It would be nice to celebrate New Year's with her.

He felt a gentle bump against his side and looked over at Evie.

"You still with me?" She smiled up at him.

"Yes, sorry. Mind wandering a bit. What were we saying?"

"How I should meet more people." Her smile widened."I feel like I've met so many people since I got here. Hope I can keep all of you straight."

He winked at her. "Just remember, I'm the one who lives next door to you."

"Ah, then I'll probably remember you," she teased.

They danced and chatted with people and he introduced her all around. She charmed everyone she met. As the dance ended, they headed outside into the night with a million stars thrown overhead.

She turned to him. "I had the best time."

"I did too." He just barely stopped himself from reaching out and sweeping one of those soft curls away from the face. The curls that had been taunting him all night. Instead, he opened the truck door for her and helped her inside, catching a glimpse of her long, lean legs as she settled into the seat.

He hurried around to the driver's side and got in. He wasn't sure how the front seat of the truck had gotten so small. He swore it had though. As though it was the most intimate space in the world with the low lights of the dashboard gently illuminating them.

They drove to her cottage in silence, with Evie engrossed in looking at all the decorations they passed. He pulled into her drive and came around to help her out. She took his offered hand and slid out, landing right against him.

She laughed gently. "Whoops. Hard to get out of the truck gracefully in these heels."

He still had her in his arms. Right, he should probably let her go. Reluctantly, he stepped back. He followed her up the porch steps and stood by her side.

"Thanks for asking me. And introducing me to so many people."

"So very many," he teased. "Just remember which one I am."

"Oh, I think I'll remember you." Her eyes locked with his.

A look that made him lose all rational thought. The world faded away as he found himself captivated by her lips, yearning to close the distance between his lips and hers.

His mind raced, debating whether he should take the chance and kiss her. The moment stretched out, electric with possibility.

Suddenly, Evie's voice cut through his thoughts. "And early tomorrow we're still on for delivering the cookies to the festival?"

He blinked, struggling to process her words.

"Randy?" she prompted gently.

"Yes, the cookies," he managed as his thoughts snapped back to reality. "I'll be over bright and early."

"Okay. See you then. Night, Randy." With a smile that left him breathless, she slipped inside, and the opportunity to kiss her vanished into the night.

Left alone on the porch, he felt the weight of

the missed moment. But he'd see her soon. First thing in the morning. He whistled under his breath as he walked over to his cottage.

CHAPTER 11

Evie woke with the sun, filled with anticipation for the festival. As she moved about the kitchen, humming a cheerful tune, she carefully arranged the cookie tins into boxes for easy transport. The irony of her newfound Christmas spirit wasn't lost on her—hadn't she sworn to ignore the holiday this year? Yet here she was, caught up in the festive whirlwind.

Her mind drifted back to the previous night's Christmas dance, a warm glow spreading through her chest. The faces of so many welcoming islanders flashed through her mind, but one stood out above the rest. Randy. Dancing with him had been… unexpected. Wonderful. She could almost feel his arms around her, the warmth of his body close to hers.

"Oh, Nana," she murmured, a smile tugging at her lips. "You always did know best." Her grandmother's final gift, that stunning dress, had been nothing short of perfect. It was as if Nana had known exactly what she would need, even from beyond.

A knock at the door pulled her from her thoughts. Her heart skipped as she hurried to answer, pausing briefly to check her reflection. The kitchen must have been warmer than she realized—a rosy flush colored her cheeks.

She opened the door to find Randy, his face split by a wide, infectious grin. "It's been forever since I've seen you," he teased, punctuating the statement with a playful wink that made her pulse quicken.

She returned his smile. "Yes, it has. Have you calculated the exact number of minutes?"

"Ah, sadly, no. I'm woefully lacking in the math department." He pressed a hand to his chest in mock distress. "But it feels like days. Weeks, even."

His playful dramatics pulled a laugh from her. "Well then," she said, stepping aside, "we'd better remedy that right away. Come on in."

He swung his hand from behind his back and held up a bag. "Today it's strawberry muffins."

She laughed. "You know, you don't have to bring me breakfast every day."

"But I like to. Besides, then I get a good breakfast too. I'm kind of tired of my usual cold cereal."

She poured them coffee and got out plates—it was getting to be a familiar routine—and they sat down at the kitchen table.

Evie savored the sweet, tangy flavor of the strawberry muffin and enjoyed the comfortable silence that had settled between her and Randy. As she sipped her coffee, she found herself studying him over the rim of her mug. His presence in her grandmother's kitchen felt so natural, as if he'd always been a part of her mornings here.

"These muffins are delicious," she said, breaking the quiet. "I might have to start bribing you to bring them every day."

He chuckled, his eyes twinkling. "No bribery necessary. I'm happy to be your personal muffin delivery service."

As they finished their breakfast, her gaze drifted to the Christmas box on the counter.

"Should we open another item before we head to the festival?" she asked.

"I think we should."

She retrieved the box and set it on the kitchen table. "It's your turn to pick," she insisted.

He reached into the box and pulled out a flat item. He handed it to her. "Here, now you unwrap it."

She carefully unwrapped the tissue paper and pulled out an old, worn postcard. The edges were frayed, and the image on the front had faded with time, but she could still make out a quaint seaside scene.

"Look at this," she said, turning it over in her hands. "It's so old."

He leaned in closer, his shoulder brushing against hers. "What does it say?"

Dear Mrs. Rogers,

I just wanted to wish you Merry Christmas and let you know that you were my favorite teacher. You taught me so much more than just book learning. You taught me life lessons and kindness and to appreciate the simple moments in life.

I hope you're enjoying living on the mainland now. You are missed here on the island.

Merry Christmas,

William Chancey

She gasped softly as the name registered. "William Chancey… that was my grandfather."

Randy's eyebrows shot up. "Really? It's from your grandfather?"

She nodded, her throat tight with emotion. "He passed away when I was very young. I barely remember him, but Nana… she always spoke of him with such love in her voice."

She ran her finger over the signature, feeling a connection to the grandfather she'd never really known. "I wonder what the story is behind this postcard. Why Nana ended up with a postcard that grandfather wrote so long ago."

"Now that's something I think I can help you with." He took the postcard and examined it. "Miss G told me a story once when I asked her about William."

"What did she say?"

"She told me about a teacher who came over from the mainland to visit William when he was dying. She showed Miss G a postcard and said she'd kept it all these years to remind herself during the rough moments that she was making a difference in the world with her teaching. She gave the postcard to Miss G to remind her that William had made such a difference in her life too by writing to her."

"We just never know the ripples of our actions, do we?" she said softly. "What a wonderful story. No wonder Nana kept it in this box with the other items she treasured."

"We don't," he agreed. His eyes met hers, filled with understanding.

She turned to face him fully, overwhelmed by gratitude. "I'm really glad you're sharing this with me," she said, her voice thick with emotion. "The opening up of each item and trying to discover why she kept it. Thank you. It means a lot to me."

He took her hand with a gentle, reassuring touch. "It means a lot to me too," he said, his voice low and sincere. "Miss G was a very special lady. And, honestly, I'm thoroughly enjoying this."

She stared down at her hand in his, feeling the connection and reluctant to break it. He finally loosened his grip and slipped his hand away, then cleared his throat. "Well, I guess we should get those cookies to the festival, don't you think?"

"Yes, we should." She stood and the intimate moment was broken.

CHAPTER 12

Evie and Randy arrived at the festival grounds, each carrying a box full of cookie tins. As they approached the bake sale booth, a wave of emotion washed over Evie. She paused, her grip tightening on the box.

Tally, who was arranging a display of gingerbread men, looked up and greeted them with a warm smile. "Evie! Randy! I'm so glad you made it." Her eyes widened as she noticed the boxes they were carrying. "Are those…?"

Evie nodded, swallowing the lump in her throat. "Nana's sugar cookies. We found her recipe and thought it would be nice to share them at the festival, just like she used to."

Randy gently squeezed her arm in support.

"It's a special recipe," he added, placing his box on the table. "We found out that Miss G got it from an old bakery here in town. These cookies have been a part of the festival for years."

"I never knew that. That's wonderful. I'm sure everyone will be thrilled to have a taste of Genevieve's famous cookies again."

Evie carefully set her box down and began taking out the cookie tins. Randy's presence beside her as he helped was reassuring.

Word quickly spread that Genevieve's sugar cookies were available at the bake sale booth. A crowd began to gather, eager to get a taste of the beloved treat. She watched in amazement as people exclaimed over the cookies, sharing their own memories of Genevieve.

A woman approached the booth, her eyes misty with nostalgia. "I heard you brought Genevieve's cookies. I'm Dorothy. Genevieve was a great friend of mine. I miss her dearly. She was one of The Yarnies, our local knitting group. I must buy a tin of her cookies."

She felt a rush of emotion at the woman's words. She glanced at Randy, who gave her an encouraging smile. "Thank you. It means a lot to hear that. Nana loved this festival and being a part of the community. And she sure loved to knit."

"That she did." Dorothy nodded.

Randy wrapped an arm around her shoulders. "You're doing a wonderful thing, sharing the cookies. Your grandmother would be so proud of you."

She leaned into his embrace, grateful for his support and the shared memories they had uncovered together from the items in Nana's Christmas box. Now the whole town knew the history behind Nana's recipe.

Randy thoroughly enjoyed watching Evie's face light up at the sights and sounds as they wandered around the festival. The twinkling lights, the garlands, and the cheerful music all seemed to captivate her, and he found himself wishing that she would fall in love with Belle Island just as deeply as he had.

As they strolled through the crowd, their hands brushed against each other, sending a shimmer of electricity through him. On impulse, he gently took her hand in his, intertwining their fingers. To his relief and delight, she didn't pull away. Instead, she gave his hand a gentle squeeze, and they continued walking hand in hand.

Her hand fit in his as if they were meant to be together. He glanced at her, admiring the way the soft glow of the Christmas lights illuminated her features, making her look even more beautiful than usual.

"This is amazing," Evie breathed, her eyes wide with wonder. "I had no idea the festival would still seem so magical."

"It's one of my favorite festivals of the year. And believe me, we have a *lot* of festivals." He laughed. "There's just something about the way the whole town comes together to celebrate at this festival that makes it extra special."

"I can see why. It's like stepping into a Christmas card or one of those feel-good Christmas movies that always have a happy ending."

He barely dared to hope this one would have a happy ending too. That maybe, just maybe, Evie would decide to stay on the island. But he had to remind himself that she'd never said one word about staying. Not one word. So he pushed the thought away.

As they made their way through the festival, he introduced Evie to various townspeople. Many of them recognized her as Genevieve's granddaughter and offered their condolences, but they also welcomed her with open arms like she was already a part of the community.

Throughout the afternoon, Randy found himself drawn to Evie's side, their hands remaining clasped together as if it were the most natural thing in the world. He reveled in the warmth of her touch and the way her laughter seemed to fill the air around them.

The festival was packed with booths full of local craftsmanship and holiday cheer, and he was charmed by her delight at looking at them all. He guided her from booth to booth, introducing her to the artisans and their wares. They paused to admire the intricate, hand-carved replicas of the island's iconic lighthouse, each one a miniature work of art. Her eyes lit up at each new discovery.

At The Yarnies' booth, he explained how the group of local knitters had come together years ago, turning their hobby into a force for good in the community. Evie ran her fingers over the soft, colorful creations—scarves, baby sweaters, and blankets—all made with love and destined to support various island charities.

As they wound their way through the crowd, the aroma of holiday treats beckoned them with a siren call. He led her to booths piled high with homemade pies, cookies, and candies. He watched with amusement as she deliberated over which sweets to try, her nose crinkling adorably as she weighed her options.

And then that wayward thought came again. He realized he wanted to do this again with her. Next year, and every year. Share the traditions of the island with her.

Luckily, at that moment, she spied the funnel cake booth and tugged on his hand. "Come on. We have to get one to split. I always got one with Nana."

When they finally got their funnel cake, she didn't hesitate to dig in. Powdered sugar drifted down on her shirt like a dusting of snow, but she was too engrossed in the moment to notice. He was captivated by her obvious delight as she savored each bite of the warm, crispy treat.

After they'd finished, he reached out without thinking. Gently, he wiped a smudge of powdered sugar from her cheek, his fingers lingering for just a moment longer than necessary.

She smiled up at him. "They are messy, but I sure love them."

Who knew that sharing a funnel cake could be such an intimate moment?

As dusk fell, he led her to the town square for the tree-lighting ceremony. He navigated them through the crowd, his hand gently guiding her by the small of her back until they reached his favorite spot. It was the perfect vantage point, offering an unobstructed view of the towering Christmas tree that stood at the center of the square.

"This is the best place to watch from," he said, leaning close to her ear so she could hear him over the excited chatter of the crowd. "You'll be able to see everything from here."

She looked up at him, her eyes sparkling with anticipation. "I can't wait. I've always loved the tree-lighting ceremony. It was one of my favorite parts of coming to visit Nana during the holidays."

And he felt lucky to be sharing the tradition with her now. As the countdown to the lighting began, she slipped her hand into his, her fingers intertwining with his own. He glanced down at their joined hands, marveling at how natural it felt.

He gave her hand a gentle squeeze, feeling the warmth of her skin against his. As she squeezed back, he felt a surge of connection between them, a sense of shared joy and anticipation.

The crowd began to chant in unison, their voices rising with each number. "Ten, nine, eight…"

His heart raced as the countdown neared its end. He turned to look at Evie, wanting to see her reaction when the tree lit up.

"Three, two, one… Lights!"

The tree burst into a dazzling display of color, the lights twinkling and shimmering against the dark night sky. She gasped, her free hand flying to her mouth in wonder. He couldn't take his eyes off her. She was stunning, her face alight with pure, childlike joy. He was certain his view was better than the view of the tree…

The crowd began to disperse, but still they stood there, hand in hand. He never wanted this moment to end. Standing there with Evie, surrounded by the magic of the Christmas season, he felt a sense of contentment and belonging that he hadn't experienced in a long time.

Evie sat out on her deck in the darkness, snuggled in Nana's favorite wrap after Randy dropped her off. The stars winked and twinkled above, along with the reliable march of the waves rolling to shore. She needed time to unwind. To think about all that had happened today. It had been magical, full of cherished memories of Nana, along with new memories being made.

Each story shared about her grandmother had filled her heart to overflowing. She missed Nana so much, but it helped to hear what an impact she'd made on so many people. As she gazed out over the moonlit water, she found herself smiling, grateful for the unexpected gifts this day had brought—connection, laughter, and a deeper appreciation for the legacy her grandmother had left behind.

And then there was Randy. Spending all that time with him. That had been… magical too. She smiled at the memory of his warm laugh and the way his eyes crinkled at the corners when he smiled. It was getting harder to deny that she was beginning to have feelings for him. The flutter in her chest whenever he was near was becoming impossible to ignore.

But it was kind of pointless, wasn't it? She'd be leaving soon. She wasn't even sure she'd stay through the holidays if she could get things wrapped up here at the cottage. The practical side of her brain insisted she really should get back home and concentrate on finding a new job.

Yet a small part of her heart whispered that maybe, just maybe, there was something worth exploring here on Belle Island. She pushed the thought away, trying to focus on the tasks ahead. She was here to sort through Nana's things.

But the task of going through all of Nana's belongings crushed her very soul. The absence of Nana's presence during the holiday season left an ache that seemed impossible to soothe. Yet even in the middle of the sadness, there was joy. The surprise of the Christmas box. That was an unexpected blessing. Getting to know so many things about Nana that she hadn't known. And sharing it with Randy made it extra special.

But reality intruded on her thoughts like a cold wave splashing over her. Her time here on the island was limited. And Randy knew she was leaving soon. So there was no reason to think that he had any kind of feelings for her beyond friendship. Friends. That was how she should think of him too.

If only she could convince her heart to think of him in that way…

CHAPTER 13

Evie felt a twinge of disappointment that she tried to ignore when Randy didn't show up the next morning. She'd gotten used to him coming over early each day to share breakfast and open a new item from the Christmas box.

To fill the void, she meandered through the cottage, sorting through belongings—some destined for packing, others for discarding. The silence hovering in every nook and cranny eventually became too much for her, and she decided to go to Magic Cafe and grab breakfast.

As she entered the cafe, Tally gave her a big hug. "There you are. Did you have a good time last night at the tree-lighting ceremony?"

"I did. It was as wonderful as I remembered

from when I used to spend Christmas here. I hadn't realized how much I missed the island."

Tally's eyes twinkled knowingly. "The island has a way of doing that. It wraps you in its charm, tugging back old memories. Welcoming you back, reminding you just how magical it is."

"I'm beginning to believe that. I'm finding it harder and harder to imagine leaving here again." There, she finally voiced the thought that had been twirling in her mind. Staying here on Belle Island.

"Well, that's simple enough," Tally said with a grin. "You should stay. You certainly have a lovely place to live."

She hesitated. "But I work in tech. There aren't many high-tech jobs here on the island. So I'm not sure how it would work."

"Bet you could find a way to make it work." Tally nodded encouragingly as she led her to a table and handed her a menu. "We always do if it's something we really want."

She sipped her coffee as she thought about what Tally said. Was Tally right? Could she make it work to stay here on the island?

And then there was Randy. If she stayed here, she would have the chance to figure out just what her feelings were for him.

But still, was it a smart decision?

Evie stirred her coffee absently, her mind churning with possibilities. The idea of staying on Belle Island tugged at her heart, but practicality warred with emotion. She'd built a life in the city with a good career—albeit without a job in hand right now. Could she really walk away from all that?

She glanced around the cafe, taking in the now familiar faces of locals starting their day. It struck her how quickly she'd fallen into the rhythm of island life. The thought both comforted and unsettled her.

Her fingers traced the worn edge of the table, a remnant of countless conversations and shared meals. The decision before her felt monumental.

As she debated the pros and cons of a major life change, she caught sight of a familiar figure entering the cafe. Julie walked up to her table with Tally at her side.

"Hi, Julie. Hope you don't mind. I'm cheating on you and having breakfast at Tally's today." She smiled up at Julie.

Julie's eyes widened in mock offense. "Tally, I hope you're not trying to steal my new favorite customer."

"Hey, you're coming for breakfast here today too." Tally shook her head.

"Right, there is that." Julie grinned.

Evie smiled, feeling a surge of affection for both women. It amazed her how quickly she'd come to care for these island residents, how easily they'd welcomed her into their circle. A sense of belonging tugged at her, making her impending decision feel even more weighty.

"Evie is thinking about staying on the island," Tally said.

"Really?" Julie turned to her.

"I'm thinking about it. I'm finding it hard to imagine leaving."

"That's how I felt when I came here as a young girl. Tally helped me out. Gave me a job. I saved and eventually opened The Sweet Shoppe. I never would have made it without Tally's help." Julie shrugged. "And a bit of the island's magic, I guess. I made a wish at Lighthouse Point and it came true."

"They do that." Tally laughed.

"I'm just not sure I can make it work…" She frowned.

"You can make it work if you want it enough," Julie said.

She smiled softly. "That's just what Tally said to me."

Tally and Julie left, and she sat eating her breakfast. She looked out at the water with the waves rolling to shore, the birds soaring overhead, and the sun sparkling on the water.

How could she leave here? And leave all her memories of spending time here with Nana? She'd still have to figure it all out. See if it was even possible. And then… there was the problem of finding a job. She'd certainly need to find work.

But she knew she wanted to try to make it happen. She wanted to stay. Deep inside her, she knew she'd never be completely happy if she left. The island was a part of her.

Evie opened the door later that morning to find Randy standing there. "Did you already open the next item from the box?"

"Of course not. Not without you. Come in." She tugged on his hand, leading him inside and into the kitchen.

"Sorry, I got tied up with a call this morning."

"That's okay. I decided to go to Magic Cafe for breakfast and... I had an interesting discussion with Tally and Julie."

"Really? What about?" He settled onto a kitchen chair.

She sat across from him and hesitated.

"Are you going to tell me?" He tilted his head.

"Yes... it's just all so new. But anyway..." She plunged on. "I'm thinking about staying here on the island. If I can work it out," she quickly added.

His eyes lit up. "You're staying?"

"Well, I'd have to figure out if I can. I'd have to find a job. And being in tech it's not like there's a lot of need for high-tech on the island."

"But we could use a lot of low-tech. Or whatever you want to call it. The city hall system goes down at least once a month, taking down the town website. We keep trying to get funding for a better system. And you saw Etta fighting with her computer system at the historical society."

"That's not exactly the kind of tech that I do anymore." She frowned.

"But you know how to do it?"

"Some. But it's been a long time."

"Or you could do something totally different. Look at Julie becoming a baker and opening The Sweet Shoppe. Or Tally with Magic Cafe. Oh, and Susan never ran an inn before she came back to the island to run Belle Island Inn. People seem to find the right career when they settle here." He leaned across the table and took her hand. "And… I'd really like it if you stayed."

She looked deep into his eyes, seeing the sincerity. "I could at least try, couldn't I? It's not like the city won't be there if I can't find something that works here. Tally said if I really want to stay, I'll find a way."

"That Tally is a wise woman."

"And I admit, I'm just not ready to leave the island. I frankly can't imagine leaving."

"Good. I'm glad you find it hard to leave. That works in my favor." He winked at her.

She laughed and stood up. "Let me get the box and we'll open another item." There was plenty enough time to figure out the logistics of staying here. For now, she'd just enjoy the holidays.

She brought the box to the table. "Whose turn is it to open one?"

"Yours."

She reached into the box and grabbed the first item her hand found. She took it out and unwrapped it. "Look, it's another ornament. A photo frame." She looked carefully at the image. "It's two little girls. And I'm pretty sure this one is Nana." She pointed to one of the girls in the picture.

Randy peered at it. "They look to be about five or so, don't they?"

"I guess so. I wonder who the other girl is?"

"I don't know. I kind of remember seeing it on her tree though. She never said anything about it." He frowned, staring hard at the photo.

"I don't know how we'll figure this one out."

"Might be another unanswerable like Fred and Lula of the music box."

"But I want to figure them all out." She shook her head. "I guess I'm greedy. Or selfish. I should be happy we've discovered why she kept so many of the pieces."

"It has been interesting to find out more about Miss G, but I guess we'll have to be content with what we've found out so far."

"I hope we have better luck tomorrow." She chased away the sense of defeat of not knowing who the other girl was in the photo.

Randy stood. "Well, I've got to go. I've got a bunch of work to catch up on today that needs to be finished."

"I won't keep you then." She rose and walked him to the door.

After he left, she stood alone in the cottage at loose ends. She could pack up more of Nana's things. But now that she wasn't going to sell it, there seemed to be no hurry.

Wait? What? Had she decided? Was she really staying? Her lips broke into a wide smile. Yes. The decision was made. She was staying. And just like Tally said, she'd find a way to make it work.

Late that afternoon, as the sun dipped lower in the sky, Evie found herself drawn to Lighthouse Point. It was Nana's favorite place on the island.

As she approached the towering structure, memories flooded back of picnics on sunny days, stargazing on clear nights, and countless conversations that had shaped her life. How many times had she come here with Nana? Too many to count. Her heart and mind filled with the joy and warmth of those memories.

She stood on the beach beneath the lighthouse as her gaze swept across the horizon, where the sky met the sea in a hazy line. The rhythmic sound of waves against the shore matched the beating of her heart.

"Nana, I'm going to stay here on the island. I want to stay here."

As a gentle breeze caressed her face, she could almost sense Nana's presence. With a surge of certainty, she knew that Nana would have approved of her decision.

As she shifted her weight, something caught her eye. She bent down and plucked a perfectly formed white cat's paw shell from the sand. Turning it over in her hand, she marveled at its delicate ridges and smooth interior. The shell felt cool against her skin as she closed her fingers around it.

"Make it possible for me to stay. To find a job. To live here on Belle Island. Make it all work out if it's meant to be," she said softly as the breeze carried her words, filled with hope, out over the sea.

Taking a deep breath, she drew back her arm and sent the shell soaring through the air. It arced gracefully before disappearing beneath the shimmering surface of the water with a soft splash, carrying her wishes out to sea.

CHAPTER 14

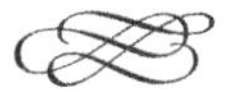

Evie hummed to herself as she moved about the kitchen, the rich aroma of freshly brewed coffee filling the air. The morning sunlight streamed through the windows and spilled across the familiar space. She breathed in deeply, a simple moment that reminded her so much of lazy mornings with Nana. And soon, this would be hers. As Tally had said, she'd find a way if she really wanted it.

As she reached for a mug, a sharp knock at the door made her pause and a smile tugged at her lips. Randy, no doubt, coming by with his usual morning treat and to open another item from the Christmas box.

She hurried to the door, her bare feet padding softly across the worn wooden floor.

She smoothed her hair quickly, then reached for the doorknob, ready to greet Randy with a warm smile.

But as the door swung open, her smile faltered. Instead of Randy's friendly face, she found herself face-to-face with a stern-looking man in a crisp suit. His expression was impassive, almost cold, and he clutched a sleek leather briefcase in one hand.

"Good morning," the man said, his voice as stiff as his posture. "Are you Genevieve Chancey?"

Her breath caught. "Ah no, that's my grandmother."

"I need to see her." It was more a command than a request.

"She's…" She swallowed. "I'm sorry. She's passed away."

A brief startled look slipped across the man's face, but he recovered quickly. "I see. And are you her heir?"

"Why are you asking?" A sense of unease crept over her.

"My name is Dexter Barlowe," he said, not bothering to offer his hand. "I need to speak with you about a matter of some importance. Since Mrs. Chancey is gone, I should talk to you if you are her granddaughter. May I come in?"

She hesitated, her hand tightening on the doorknob. Everything about this man set her on edge—his formal attire was so out of place on the island, and his businesslike demeanor seemed to chill the warm morning air. But curiosity mingled with her apprehension.

"I… suppose so," she said finally, stepping back to allow him entry. "Please, come in."

She closed the door behind him, wishing fervently that it had been Randy at the door instead.

She led Mr. Barlowe into the living room, her mind racing. The cozy space now seemed small and confining. She gestured for him to take a seat on the couch while she perched on the edge of Nana's chair, her back straight and tense.

Mr. Barlowe settled himself, placing his briefcase on the coffee table. His eyes darted around the room, taking in the weathered furniture and the family photos on the mantel. There was something in his gaze that made her uncomfortable. It was as if he was assessing the value of everything he saw.

"As I said, I have something important to

discuss with you." Mr. Barlowe's lips twitched in what might have been a smile, but it didn't reach his eyes. "I've recently been going through my grandfather's estate and came across something quite interesting." He reached into his briefcase and pulled out a leather portfolio. He carefully extracted an old, yellowed document. The paper looked fragile, its edges slightly frayed with age.

"What is that?" She eyed him suspiciously.

"This," he said, holding up the document, "is a loan agreement between my grandfather and yours."

Her eyes widened in surprise. "A loan agreement?"

He nodded, his expression grave. "It appears that your grandfather, William, borrowed a significant sum from my grandfather many years ago. And according to this document, he used this very cottage as collateral."

The words hit her like a physical blow. She felt the blood drain from her face as she struggled to process what she was hearing. "That... that can't be right," she stammered. "I've never heard anything about a loan."

"I'm afraid it is," he replied, his tone matter-of-fact. "And according to the terms of the agreement, the full amount is now due."

Her heart pounded in her chest. This couldn't be happening. Not now, not when she had just decided to make this place her home. "May I… may I see the document?" she asked, struggling to hide the panic rising inside her.

Mr. Barlowe handed her the yellowed papers. She took them, her hands trembling slightly as she unfolded them. She scanned the faded typewritten words, seeing her grandfather's signature at the bottom. The amount listed made her eyes widen in disbelief.

As the reality of the situation sank in, she felt as if the floor had dropped out from beneath her. The cottage, her inheritance, her newfound dream of staying on Belle Island—it all seemed to be slipping away in an instant.

"I'll need to have a lawyer look over these documents," she said, forcing her voice to sound stronger than she felt.

Mr. Barlowe nodded, his expression unchanged. "Of course. I've made you a copy." He reached into his briefcase and pulled out a manila envelope, handing it to her while taking back the original document.

She accepted the envelope, her fingers

gripping it tightly. "Thank you," she said, though gratitude was the last thing she felt at that moment.

Mr. Barlowe cleared his throat, then continued in his businesslike tone. "I should inform you that I'm legally entitled to collect the full amount immediately or take possession of the cottage. My lawyers have thoroughly examined the document."

Her heart sank even further. "And how long do I have to… to figure this out?"

"I'm giving you a deadline of two weeks to repay the loan," Mr. Barlowe stated flatly.

The room spun around her. Two weeks? How could she possibly come up with that kind of money in just fourteen days? She swallowed hard, trying to keep her composure.

"Mr. Barlowe," she began, her voice trembling slightly despite her best efforts, "is there any way we could negotiate? Or maybe extend the deadline? This is all so sudden, and I—"

"I'm afraid not," he cut her off, his tone leaving no room for argument. "I've already waited far too long to claim what's rightfully mine. I have no idea why my grandfather didn't collect on this debt sooner."

A flicker of anger ignited amid her panic. How could he be so cold about this? This wasn't just a piece of property to her. This was her grandmother's home, filled with memories and love.

"But this cottage," she tried again, "it's been in my family for years. My grandmother just passed away. Surely you can understand. I need some time."

Mr. Barlowe held up a hand, cutting her off once more. "I sympathize with your situation, but business is business. The terms of the agreement are clear, and I'm well within my rights to enforce them."

She fell silent, her mind frantically searching for a solution, any solution. But the reality of the situation left her feeling helpless and overwhelmed.

Mr. Barlowe stood, straightening his suit jacket. "I'll expect to hear from you or your lawyer soon." He handed her a business card. "Good day."

As he let himself out, she noticed a hint of satisfaction in his expression, as if he was already envisioning the cottage as his own. She sank back into her chair and pulled out her copy of the agreement, reading it over again.

Dropping it onto the table, she stood and walked over to the bookshelf, picking up a framed photo of Nana, remembering her grandmother's words: "You end up in life where you're supposed to be."

Maybe this meant the cottage was never truly meant to be hers.

CHAPTER 15

Randy glanced at his watch as he knocked on Evie's door. He was a little later than normal, but he'd still picked up fresh buttermilk and blueberry muffins from The Sweet Shoppe. As Evie opened the door, he immediately knew something was wrong by the look on her face.

"What? What is it?"

"I—" Her voice cracked.

He stepped inside and pulled her into his arms. "Tell me."

She clung to him for a moment before pulling back. She motioned for him to follow as she turned toward the kitchen without a word.

As they got to the kitchen, his eyes darted over the scattered papers on the table. Setting down the bag of muffins, he turned his full attention to Evie.

"What's going on?" he asked gently.

She took a shaky breath, her hands fidgeting with the edge of one of the papers. "A man came by this morning. A Mr. Barlowe. He… he says he has a legal claim to the cottage."

Randy frowned. "What do you mean, a legal claim?"

"Apparently, my grandfather used the cottage as collateral for a loan years ago," she explained, her voice breaking. "The man says the loan was never repaid."

His mind raced, trying to make sense of this new information. "But your grandmother left you the cottage. How can someone else have a claim on it?"

She shook her head. "I don't know all the details. He has all these legal documents." She gestured helplessly at the papers scattered on the table.

He moved closer. "Okay, let's take this step by step. Did he say how much is owed?"

She nodded, reaching for one of the papers. "It's all here. The original loan amount, plus years of interest. It's… it's a lot."

His stomach tightened as he saw the figure. "And how long did he say you have to repay it?"

"He said two weeks. He can't do that, can he?" she whispered, her voice barely audible. "If I can't come up with the money by then, he says he'll take possession of the cottage."

His mind whirled with questions. "Have you spoken to a lawyer? There might be some way to challenge this or at least buy more time."

She shook her head. "I haven't had a chance yet. It all happened so fast, and I'm… so overwhelmed."

He squeezed her shoulder gently. "We'll figure this out. There has to be a solution. Do you have the man's contact information? Maybe we can arrange a meeting and try to negotiate."

She nodded, rifling through the papers until she found a business card. She handed it to him and he studied it carefully.

"I think our first step is to meet with a lawyer. Call Mr. Howe, Miss G's lawyer, and show this to him."

"Yes, that's where I should start. You're right." She walked over to the counter and picked up Miss G's address book. She leafed through it, then dialed. After speaking on the phone for a few minutes, she turned to him. "I have an appointment in an hour. I explained how it's kind of an emergency."

"Try not to lose hope. We'll explore every option. We'll figure this out."

At least he hoped they would, because he'd been feeling so lucky that she'd decided to stay here on the island. Would she change her mind if she lost the cottage?

Evie felt Randy's reassuring hand on her back as he opened the door to Mr. Howe's office.

No one was at the receptionist's desk, but the door to Mr. Howe's office was wide open. They walked over to it and saw him, dressed casually in slacks and a short-sleeved knit shirt. His desk was a large, old wooden one covered in stacks of papers. One wall of the office was lined with dark mahogany shelving stuffed with books. She knocked lightly on the doorframe.

Mr. Howe looked up. "There you are. Evie, good to see you. And Randy, hello." Mr. Howe walked over and shook their hands. "Please, take a seat."

They sat across from him. "Sorry about no receptionist. I gave her some extra time off during the holiday season. She has four kids and lots to do." He smiled at them. "Now, I assume you brought the document?"

Her hands trembled slightly as she handed the document to Mr. Howe. She watched anxiously as he carefully read the paper, her stomach knotting with each passing second. When he finally looked up, his expression was serious.

"I'm afraid Mr. Barlowe's claim appears to be legally valid," Mr. Howe said, frowning.

Her heart sank. She'd known it was a possibility, but hearing it confirmed made it all too real. She struggled to keep her composure.

Randy reached over and gave her hand a reassuring squeeze. She glanced at him, managing a small, grateful smile.

Mr. Howe leaned back in his chair, tapping his pen thoughtfully against his desk. After a moment, he spoke again, a hint of optimism in his voice. "Of course, with personal loans, it's hard to prove authenticity. And at the very least, I believe I might be able to buy you more time."

Her heart leaped at his words as she clung to this tiny hope. She leaned forward eagerly. "What do you mean? How?"

The lawyer set down his pen and folded his

hands on the desk. "There are a few legal strategies we could employ to delay the process," he explained. "It's an old document and there might be technicalities we can use to our advantage. I'll also do some looking into the Barlowe family."

She nodded, her hope growing. "How long do you think you could delay it?" Not that she thought she'd be able to come up with the sum, anyway. So, eventually, she'd still lose the cottage.

Mr. Howe rubbed his chin. "It's hard to say for certain, but I'd estimate we could potentially buy you an additional two to three months, maybe even more, if we're lucky."

Evie felt a bit of relief wash over her. It wasn't a solution, but it was something. A chance. She glanced at Randy, who gave her an encouraging nod.

"Thank you. Start wherever you think is best." She wondered how much his legal fees would amount to.

"I can get started right away."

"I… I had just decided on keeping the cottage," she admitted.

A warm smile spread across the lawyer's face. "Genevieve had hoped you'd keep it."

Surprise flickered through her. Nana hadn't ever told her she wanted her to keep the cottage. "She did?"

"Yes, she did. And she told me to help you in any way I can. There will be no fees for my services. Genevieve helped me greatly when I first moved to the island. I never would have had a successful practice without her help. She was a special lady."

"She was." Evie nodded, marveling again at how Nana had quietly helped so many people.

"I'll keep in touch," Mr. Howe said as he rose.

"Thank you." Gratitude welled up inside her. "I appreciate any help you can give me."

She and Randy walked out into the bright sunshine. He turned to her. "See, there's hope."

She took a deep breath, tilting her face toward the sky, allowing the sun to wash over her, then looked at Randy. "A little hope is better than none." She allowed herself to believe, just for a moment, that everything might work out after all.

Evie invited Randy over later that evening to open another item from the Christmas box. They settled on the couch with the box on the table. The lights from her Christmas tree cast a warm, cheerful glow around them. She'd put on Bing Crosby's White Christmas album, another one of her favorites.

"You pick. I like watching you choose." He smiled at her, his eyes filled with warmth and… and something.

She opened the box and reached inside, then unwrapped her chosen item to find a small velvet pouch. She loosened the drawstring and pulled out a small piece of glass. "Oh, it's sea glass. And it looks just like a Christmas tree, doesn't it?"

He took it from her and inspected it. "It does look like a Christmas tree."

"How will we ever figure out why she had this?"

"Now this time, I'm not sure. Maybe she found it?"

"Maybe. But it seems like all the items have a deeper meaning than just something she found and liked, doesn't it?"

"I guess so."

"Maybe this is another one we won't find

out about, just like we don't know who that little girl is in that photo ornament with Nana or who Fred and Lula are." She had to admit she was getting a little discouraged that they weren't doing very well with figuring out why Nana kept some of the items.

He looked over at her. "You okay?"

She attempted a smile. "I'm fine. It's just been a really long day."

He stood up. "I should go. Let you get some rest."

She rose. "I'm probably lousy company now, anyway."

He reached out and touched her cheek, running his finger across it lightly. "You are never lousy company." He took her hand as they walked to the door.

He paused at the door, wrapped his arms around her, and held her close. "It's going to be okay. You'll see."

As he slowly stroked her back, she could almost—almost—believe his words.

Almost.

He pulled back and gazed at her intently, his eyes searching hers. Her breath caught in her throat and her pulse quickened.

Was he going to kiss her?

The moment stretched between them, charged with unspoken possibility. But then his expression softened into a small, lopsided smile that made her heart skip a beat. Without a word, he turned and walked out the door, leaving her standing there with both disappointment and longing swirling inside of her.

As she watched him go, she wondered what might have happened if he had stayed just a moment longer.

Though maybe she'd read the situation wrong. Maybe he hadn't wanted to kiss her.

But did she *want* him to kiss her?

Everything in her life was so up in the air right now. Just a day after she thought she'd had things figured out.

She turned and looked around the room. Even the Christmas decorations and pretty lights couldn't hide the stack of packing boxes mocking her in the corner of the room.

Uneasiness settled on her shoulders. Should she go ahead and keep packing? Because if she lost the cottage, she'd have to have all this sorted out.

But she didn't have the heart to attempt it

tonight. She flicked off the lights and headed to bed, hoping to escape into a book.

CHAPTER 16

Evie woke up early the next morning, determined to at least sort through more of Nana's things. They would need sorting out no matter if she stayed here or left the island. She'd barely slept, tossing and turning, as worrying about the cottage's future haunted her dreams. She quickly got dressed and went to the kitchen to grab a cup of coffee. With cup in hand, she headed to the storage closet.

She stood back, taking in all the shelves spread out before her. She set the cup on a shelf and pulled out a small, sturdy stepladder. Placing it near the furthest shelving unit, she slowly climbed up the steps and reached up to the top shelf to grab a large box. Carefully balancing it on her hip, she climbed down the ladder.

The box was labeled: Important Papers. But it wasn't her grandmother's writing. Maybe her grandfather's? She tucked the box under one arm, carried her coffee with the other hand, and headed to the kitchen so she'd have better light. She set the box on the table and pulled off the lid. Inside was a small metal box with a lock on it.

Now how would she figure out how to open it? She scowled at it, thinking. She tried the street address. No luck. Her grandmother's birthday. No luck. Then she paused and slowly tried her birthday. The box opened wide for her.

The documents inside were old and crinkled. She sifted through the papers, opening each one and glancing at it. Near the bottom of the stack was a yellowed, typewritten document. As she unfolded it, her heart sank. It was an exact copy of the document Mr. Barlowe had shown her, signed by her grandfather. A handwritten note tumbled out that simply said "loan from Bart Barlowe."

She knew in her heart that this proved that the Barlowes' claim was valid. She dropped onto the chair. Why hadn't Nana told her? Did she even know?

This changed everything. If it was a debt to be paid, it needed to be paid. Her brief hope of staying here in the cottage on the island crumbled into tiny grains of sand.

Her phone rang, startling her from her thoughts. She glanced at the caller ID and saw it was Mr. Howe, the lawyer. Her heart raced as she answered.

"Hello, Mr. Howe," she said, trying to keep her voice steady.

"Hello, Evie. I'm calling about the situation with your grandmother's cottage." His voice carried a note of hesitation. "I've been looking into the matter, but I'm having a hard time disproving the validity of the document Mr. Barlowe showed you."

She took a deep breath. "It's valid," she said quietly. "I found my grandfather's copy of it in an old lockbox. There's no doubt about it now."

There was a pause on the other end of the line. "I see," Mr. Howe said finally. "That does change things."

"I'll need to pay back the debt. It's what Nana would want me to do."

"Are you sure about this, Evie?" Mr. Howe

asked. "There might still be other options we could explore."

"No, I'm sure. It's the right thing to do. Nana always taught me to honor our commitments."

"But if you don't have the funds to pay him back, he'll get Genevieve's cottage," he warned.

"I know. But I don't see another way out. I don't have that kind of money." Maybe if she sold the cottage, she'd have the money, but either way, she'd lose the cottage.

"I'm sorry. I know Genevieve would have loved for you to stay and live in her cottage," he said, his voice filled with kindness and empathy.

"Do you think Nana knew about this loan?"

"I have to think not, because she was very precise about her wishes with her will. I don't think she would have ignored this."

"You're probably right. Anyway, thank you, Mr. Howe. I appreciate all your help."

After hanging up, she sat at the kitchen table, staring at the documents spread out before her. The reality was sinking in. She was losing the cottage.

She picked up her coffee mug, now cold, and walked to the window. The view of the island, with its gentle waves lapping at the shore, had always brought her comfort. Now, it felt more like she was seeing it for the last time, and the view was slowly slipping away.

Her phone pinged with incoming emails. At first she ignored them, but then she sighed and opened her phone to check them. A reminder that her rent was due back home. Two spam emails. And one from… Totten Technologies. Wasn't that the company where she'd met the woman—Kristine, was it?—at a networking event she'd gone to right before she came here? The woman was smart, talented, and seemed interested in her, but had no openings at Totten for Evie's skill set. Kristine had requested her resume and said she'd keep it on file. But isn't that what people always say?

She clicked on the email and read it, her eyes widening. Kristine had an opening she thought would be perfect for Evie. She'd checked out her references and was impressed by the jobs she'd held. Kristine was on board with hiring her. She just had to formally get the okay from human resources. She wanted to arrange an interview as soon as possible.

She leaned against the counter, stunned. It couldn't possibly be that easy to get a new job, could it? And Totten was one of the top technology companies in Baltimore.

It was like everything was giving her a sign that she should leave. The loan against the cottage, the almost job offer back home.

Her heart was breaking at the thought of leaving and losing the cottage, but maybe all these things were a sign she wasn't meant to be here.

She stared out the window, not really seeing anything. Soon, someone else would be standing here in the very spot.

Not her. Not Nana.

She set her cup in the sink and headed back to the storage room. Now she had to get moving in earnest. There were things to pack up, to give away, to pitch. And the fact that she didn't want to do any of that didn't make any difference. She had to do it.

Evie heard a knock at the door, and her heart sank. She was sure it would be Randy, eager to open another item from the Christmas box. She wasn't ready to face him, to share the news that would change everything. She walked to the front room, took a deep breath, steeled herself, and opened the door.

Randy stood there, as expected, his face lit up with a warm smile. "Hey there! Ready for today's Christmas box adventure?" He held up a thermos. "I brought some hot cocoa to go with it."

Evie tried to manage a smile but knew it wouldn't fool him. "Come in." She stepped aside to let him enter.

Randy's smile faded as he looked at her. "Everything okay? Did you hear more from the lawyer?"

"Yes… I… Come in and sit."

She led him to the living room, where boxes were stacked haphazardly. The Christmas box sat on the coffee table, untouched. She perched on the edge of the couch, her hands clasped tightly.

"I… I need to tell you something." She took a shaky breath. "I've decided to leave Belle Island."

His face fell, the sparkle in his eyes gone. "Leave? But I thought… What about staying here? Living in your grandmother's cottage?"

She tried to explain. "I can't keep the cottage. I found a copy of the loan papers in my grandfather's things with a handwritten note. The loan is real. I have to repay the debt. It's what Nana would want me to do." She looked down at her hands.

"But there must be some way—" he started, but she shook her head.

"I don't have that kind of money. And then… well, I got a job offer back home. It's with a great company. One I've always wanted to work for." She tried to inject some enthusiasm into her voice, but it fell flat.

His forehead creased into a deep frown. "So that's it? You're just going to leave?"

Her eyes filled with unshed tears. "I don't want to. But what choice do I have? This cottage was a beautiful dream, but it looks like it wasn't meant to be mine. Nana always said you end up where you're supposed to be in life."

"And you think that's not here?" His voice was low and tinged with hurt.

She looked around the room, at the boxes of memories, at the Christmas decorations they'd put up together. "I don't know anymore. Everything seems to be pushing me back home. The loan, the job offer… it feels like the universe is trying to tell me something."

He leaned forward, his elbows on his knees. "You can't just give up. You've made friends here like Tally and Julie. You said you love it here on the island. There has to be a way to keep the cottage, to stay here. We can figure something out together."

Her heart ached at the sincerity in his voice, at the way he said "we." But she shook her head.

"But what about us?" He looked deep into her eyes, and she was helpless to turn away.

"I guess we just weren't meant to be, either. Our timing was off." She tore her gaze from his. "I'm sorry. I have to go home and take this job if I get it, or another one. Earn a living. It was a beautiful dream, but realistically, it just can't happen."

He rose from his chair, his eyes a mix of anger and hurt. "So you're not even willing to try? To give us a chance? You're just leaving?"

"I—I have nothing here, Randy. No place to live, no job. And to live here on Belle Island with someone else in Nana's house?" She blinked rapidly, trying to hold back her tears. "I don't think I could take that. It would crush my very soul."

"Fine. It's clear you've made your decision."

His words were laced with icy anger. "I should go."

"Randy, wait." She jumped out and reached out a hand.

He dodged her hand and headed to the door. "Goodbye, Evie. Have a good life."

She sank onto the couch as tears began to flow. How many tears had she shed in the last month or so? More than in her whole lifetime prior to these last few rough months. She looked over at the Christmas box, ready for her to take out today's item.

But she couldn't. Not alone.

Randy sat out on his porch, the thermos of hot cocoa beside him. He poured himself a single cup and took a sip. Somehow, it didn't taste like it would have if he'd shared it with Evie.

He sat there and nursed his cup of hot cocoa until it went cold. Anger and hurt swirled inside him. He couldn't believe she was just going to leave Belle Island, leave him, after everything they'd shared.

Memories flashed through his mind. Opening Miss G's Christmas box and discovering the stories behind each item. The way Evie's eyes had sparkled with curiosity and joy, the way her laughter had filled the room. He'd felt a connection with her, a sense of belonging that he hadn't experienced in years.

But now she was leaving. Just like his ex-wife had left him all those years ago. The pain of that abandonment still stung, a wound that had never fully healed. And now, Evie's decision to go felt like another knife twisting in his heart.

Maybe it was his destiny to be alone. To watch the women he cared about walk away from him, from Belle Island. First his wife, and now Evie.

Evie had talked about the job offer, about the need to repay her grandfather's debt. But couldn't she see that there was more to life than that? That there were things worth fighting for, worth staying for? Evidently, he wasn't one of them.

He set the mug on the table beside him, the liquid sloshing over the rim. He stood up, pacing back and forth as the frustration and disappointment coursed through him. He'd thought Evie was different, that she understood the magic of Belle Island, the way it could heal a person's soul.

But maybe he'd been wrong. Maybe she was just like everyone else, always looking for something better, something more. Never content with what was right in front of her.

He had to admit, though, the anger and hurt he felt over Evie's decision to leave Belle Island warred with his desire to understand her perspective.

He knew how much the cottage meant to her, how it was tied to the memories of her grandmother. Miss G had been a constant in both their lives, someone who had welcomed them both into her heart. He could only imagine how difficult it must be for Evie to face the prospect of losing that connection.

But still, he couldn't help but feel like she was giving up too easily. Miss G had always been a fighter, a woman who faced challenges head-on. He was certain that she would have wanted Evie to do the same, to explore every possible angle before admitting defeat.

All the moments they'd shared together ran through his mind again. Decorating the cottage, baking Miss G's cookies, and the Christmas Festival. Not to mention opening all those items from the Christmas box and trying to figure out why they were special to Miss G. In those moments, he'd truly come to believe that Evie belonged on Belle Island, that this was where she was meant to be.

He looked out at the water, unable to shake the feeling that he needed to go to Evie, to try and convince her to stay and fight for the cottage. Nana would have wanted that, and deep down, he knew he wanted it too.

But what if she rejected his plea? What if his attempts to change her mind only drove her further away? He'd seen the determination in her eyes. She'd made up her mind. No, he couldn't do it. Couldn't risk rejection all over again.

He leaned against the railing, staring out at the ocean. The waves rolled to the shore, a constant rhythm that usually soothed him. But today, it only seemed to mock him, reminding him of the emptiness that awaited him.

He closed his eyes, trying to push away the memories of Evie, of the laughter and warmth they'd shared. But they clung to him, refusing to let go. Just like the hope he'd foolishly allowed himself to feel, the belief that maybe, just maybe, he'd found someone who would stay.

CHAPTER 17

Evie woke up the next morning and a sadness settled over her as soon as she remembered she was leaving. Leaving the island and Randy. She climbed out of bed and slowly pulled on her outfit, not really caring what she chose. After grabbing a cup of coffee, she headed out to the main room and settled on the couch.

Bad decision.

The Christmas box sat there on the coffee table, mocking her. She ran her finger over the carved design but couldn't bring herself to open it. There were still a few items left in the box, she knew that, but she couldn't find joy in opening them alone.

She glanced at her phone. No messages

from Randy, not that she was really expecting to hear from him. As she swept her gaze around the room, seeing the empty boxes needing to be packed, she suddenly couldn't face the task. Maybe after a good breakfast, she'd feel more like it.

But she doubted it…

She headed to Magic Cafe—anywhere to get away from the silence of the cottage and the looming boxes.

The tinkling bell above the entrance announced her arrival when she pushed open the door. The warm aroma of freshly brewed coffee and baked goods provided a momentary respite from her troubles. She scanned the cozy interior, her gaze settling on Tally, who was busy waiting on some customers.

Tally looked up, her eyes meeting hers, and a welcoming smile spread across her face. She motioned for her to take a table. She took one at the edge of the beach and stared out at the sunlight dancing on top of the waves. A sight that normally would have enchanted her, but today it was a bleak reminder of all that she was getting ready to lose.

Tally came up to the table and immediately

a frown crept over her features. "What's wrong, hon? I can see something is bothering you."

"I—" Tears threatened to spill. Again.

"I'll be right back." Tally disappeared, then returned with two steaming mugs of coffee, plunking them down on the table before sitting down across from her. "Okay, tell me what's wrong," Tally prodded, her voice laced with concern.

She took a deep breath, hoping to steady her voice. She wrapped her hands around the comforting warmth of the coffee mug. "It's the cottage," she began, her words coming out in a rush. "A man—Mr. Barlowe—showed up yesterday, claiming my grandfather had taken out a loan from his grandfather and used the cottage as collateral. He had a loan agreement and everything."

Tally leaned forward and frowned. "There were some Barlowes who lived on the island. They've been gone a long time though."

"He gave me two weeks to repay the full amount, or he'll take possession of the cottage."

"Are you sure the loan is real? It's valid?"

"It is. I found a copy in my grandfather's things. And I know that Nana would want me to pay back the loan. I don't have that kind of money… so… I'm going to lose the cottage."

Tally reached across the table and gently squeezed her hand, offering a silent gesture of support and understanding. "I'm so sorry you're going through this," she said, her voice filled with sympathy. "It must be incredibly overwhelming."

She nodded, feeling a wave of gratitude for Tally's presence and the comfort she provided. "I've been trying to find a way to stay here on Belle Island, to make the cottage my home," she confessed. "And I told Randy I was staying, and I thought we were going to have a chance to see… to see if things might work out between us. But then all this happened."

"Are you sure you can't figure something out?"

"It's hopeless. And I got a tentative job offer back in Baltimore. It's like I wasn't really meant to stay here."

"Or maybe you are. Do you have feelings for Randy?" Tally asked.

"I… I might. But even if I do, what good does that do me? I'm leaving. We'll be miles and miles apart."

"Don't give up hope yet. The island has a

way of making things work out how they're supposed to be."

"And maybe I'm supposed to go back to Baltimore." She stared at her coffee.

"You know what you need? A pick me up. How about meeting Julie and me for the annual Christmas caroling night? We all meet by the gazebo and sing Christmas carols. It's a fun time and a lovely way to celebrate the season."

"I'm afraid I wouldn't be very good company."

"That's okay. Come anyway. It will lift your spirits. It's hard to be sad and in a bad mood when you're singing carols."

She smiled weakly. "You're probably right."

"Good, then we'll see you there at seven. Bring your best singing voice." Tally smiled as she rose. "We'll be expecting you."

She was pretty sure no one ever said no to Tally. So it looked like she was going to the annual Christmas caroling night.

Evie arrived at the gathering a few minutes before seven. The gazebo was lit up with hundreds of twinkling lights, casting a magical glow around the town square. The scent of hot cocoa and freshly baked cookies wafted on the air as the townspeople gathered around, talking excitedly, waiting for the caroling to begin.

Tally waved to her, and she wove her way through the crowd to join her and Julie.

"You made it. I was afraid you'd decide not to come," Tally said, her eyes filled with concern.

"No, you were right. It will do me good to be out. No use sitting at home and feeling sorry for myself." She pasted on a smile.

"Tally told me what happened," Julie said. "I'm so sorry." She pressed a cup of hot cocoa into her hands. "Here. Take this."

"Thank you." She was grateful for the small kindness as she wrapped her hands around the warm cup.

The mayor interrupted their conversation when he went up to the gazebo. "Welcome, everyone. Glad to have you here. Now I'm going to turn us over to the high school music teacher and we'll get started."

As her gaze roamed over the crowd, she spied Randy on the other side of the gazebo, his familiar silhouette illuminated by the twinkle lights. She only allowed herself a moment to drink in the sight of him, then turned away.

The crowd started to sing "Silent Night," and she joined in. But the words caught in her throat as she remembered coming here so many times with Nana and knowing this was the last caroling night she'd go to. Her gaze kept drifting back toward Randy, who steadfastly ignored her, his jaw set in a tense line.

Tally nudged her. "Aren't those wreaths pretty on the gazebo? I swear, each year we get more and more decorations up here in the square."

"They are very pretty," she answered automatically.

Just then, the children's choir tramped up to the gazebo to sing Jingle Bells. The cheerful tune and the animated faces of the children did lift her spirits slightly. But when they finished and rushed back to their parents, the reality of her situation came crashing back.

"I'm a bit tired. I think I'll head out now," she whispered to Tally.

Tally just nodded with knowing eyes.

Evie lingered at the edge of the gathering, watching families and friends embracing the holiday spirit. The joyous atmosphere only heightened her sense of isolation. Children laughed as they chased each other around the gazebo, their parents chatting happily nearby. Couples held hands, sharing warm glances as they sipped their cocoa.

She felt like an outsider looking in, no longer part of the community she'd briefly allowed herself to imagine joining. The realization stung, reminding her of all she was about to lose.

With a final glance at Randy, who was now engrossed in conversation with other islanders, she slipped away from the square. She moved quietly, not wanting to draw attention to her departure. As much as she appreciated Tally's efforts to include her, the gathering had only proven how alone she truly was.

As she walked home alone, she passed houses adorned with twinkling lights and Christmas decorations, each display a bittersweet reminder of the life she was about to leave behind. The elaborate Santa and reindeer scene on the roof of the yellow house on the corner, the beautifully lit nativity in front of the white house with the cute picket fence, and old Mrs. Peterson's simple but elegant wreath—all sights she'd grown to love during her time on the island.

She remembered helping her grandmother put up similar decorations when she was young, the excitement she'd felt as a child seeing the island transform into a winter wonderland—albeit a warm, sandy winter wonderland. Now, those memories served as a painful reminder of all she was losing—not just her grandmother's cottage, but the chance to build a life here, to create new traditions and memories.

The walk seemed longer than usual, each step taking her further from the warmth of the community gathering and closer to the reality of her situation. The sound of carols faded behind her, replaced by the gentle lapping of waves against the shore and the distant cry of seagulls. The sounds that had become comforting to her over the past weeks but now seemed to echo her loneliness.

Reaching her grandmother's cottage, she paused on the porch, surveying the holiday decorations she'd put up. They'd all have to come down now. The cheerful glow from the lights did little to chase away the heaviness in her heart as she unlocked the door to what would soon no longer be her home.

CHAPTER 18

Evie spent the next couple of days working on packing up the cottage, not allowing herself any breaks, trying to keep busy. Because if she kept very, very busy, maybe she could forget these were her last days here at Nana's cottage.

She paused when she heard a knock at the door. With a catch in her breath, she hurried to answer, hoping it was Randy.

She opened the door to find not Randy but a woman standing there, a tentative expression on her face. The woman asked, "Is Genevieve available?"

Her heart sank. Not again. Now what? She took a deep breath and explained, "No, I'm sorry. Genevieve was my grandmother. She passed away recently."

The woman's eyes widened, and she placed a hand over her heart. "Oh, I'm so sorry for your loss. My condolences."

Her sympathy seemed genuine, and she felt a slight sense of relief. But she hoped this wasn't another person demanding payment for a long-forgotten debt.

"I'm Susan Green," the woman introduced herself. "My mother, Linda Green, was friends with Genevieve for many years."

She'd never heard Nana mention a Linda Green. "Really? I don't recall Nana mentioning your grandmother."

Susan smiled. "It's been a long time since they saw each other, but my mother always spoke fondly of Genevieve. They grew up together near Plymouth."

She hesitated for a moment, then stepped aside. "Please, come in." *Please don't tell me Nana has an outstanding loan too.*

"Can I get you something to drink? Coffee, tea?" she offered, leading Susan to the couch.

"Tea would be lovely, thank you," Susan replied, settling onto the couch. Her gaze swept around the cottage, but not like Mr. Barlowe's, evaluating everything. Susan's gaze was more approving and appreciative.

She busied herself in the kitchen, preparing two cups of tea. Her mind raced with questions about Susan's grandmother and her connection to Nana. When she returned to the living room, she handed Susan a cup and sat down beside her.

"So, tell me about your mother and Nana's friendship," she prompted, eager to learn more.

Susan cradled the warm mug in her hands. "Well, from what my mother told me, she and Genevieve grew up together. Best friends. I guess they were inseparable until Genevieve moved away to Belle Island and got married."

"Did they see each other after that?"

"They must have..." Susan put her cup down on the coffee table. "Because Genevieve helped my mother out when she needed it most."

"What do you mean?"

"My father was—let's say a *mean* man—and my mother had a rough go of it. My father finally left us, which was probably for the best. But he left my mother with nothing. No money, no home, and a young child to take care of—me."

"That's terrible."

Susan nodded. "Genevieve found out and traveled back home to see my mother. And..." Susan's voice cracked. "And she did the kindest thing. She had inherited a house that had been in her family for generations. She gave the house to my mother. Deeded it to her. Said she had no desire to ever leave Belle Island, so she didn't need a house in Plymouth to keep up with. And gave my mother money to help start up a business."

"Nana did that? She never told me."

"I don't know if you've heard of Genny Cosmetics."

"Of course I have." It was a multi-million-, maybe multi-billion-dollar company that made skincare and makeup products.

"Well, that's my mother's company. Well, mine now." The woman smiled slightly. "My mother passed away recently."

"Oh, I'm so sorry."

"Thank you. And... don't you see? The company was named after Genevieve."

"Oh, I didn't even put two and two together."

"Genevieve said the house was a gift. That she wasn't ever going to move back and she'd rather my mother have it than let it sit and fall into rubble since she was the last heir in her family. But as my mother was dying, she made me promise that the house would be sold and the proceeds go back to Genevieve. It was sold for quite a large sum. It was a beautiful lot, right on the coast. So, I guess that money is yours now."

She sat back, stunned.

"There's a bit of a tie-up with my mother's estate, but my lawyer says the funds will come through any day now."

Could it really happen? Could she have the money to pay off Mr. Barlowe and save Nana's cottage? Her heart did a double beat with hope.

"I—I don't know what to say."

Susan grinned. "Say that you'll put the money to good use."

"Oh, I will. You see, my grandfather took out a loan and they are demanding repayment now, and I was going to lose this cottage. It was breaking my heart. But now… now I have hope that I can save it if the funds come through in time."

"It looks like Genevieve's kindness is coming back to help you then, doesn't it?" Susan's eyes lit up with pleasure.

"It does."

"Well, I should go. I just wanted to come in person to meet Genevieve and thank her for her kindness. But I'll convey my gratitude to you instead. Your grandmother was a special person." Susan stood.

"She was." She started to walk Susan to the door. "Oh, wait right there for a moment."

She hurried away and returned with the framed ornament she'd unwrapped from the Christmas box. She held it out to Susan. "Any chance that this is your mom with Nana?"

Susan took the ornament and a gentle smile spread across her face. "It is. Look at them. They were so young." Tears shimmered in the corner of her eyes.

"Take it," she insisted. "Keep it as a memory of the friendship they shared and how an act of kindness can help in unexpected ways."

"Thank you. I'll treasure it." Susan walked out the door and turned back. "I'll be in touch as soon as I know something. Really, it should be any day."

Evie couldn't wait to tell Tally the good news. She still had a little over a week left to repay the loan. Surely the funds would come through by then and Nana's kindness would save the cottage.

She burst into Magic Cafe, her heart racing with excitement. She spotted Tally over by the coffee counter and rushed over, barely able to contain her smile. "Tally, you won't believe what just happened!"

Tally looked up from the coffee machine, her eyebrows raised in surprise. "What's going on? You look like you just won the lottery."

She leaned against the counter, taking a deep breath before launching into her story. "Better than the lottery. Remember how I told you about Mr. Barlowe claiming that my grandfather owed him money and that I had to pay back the loan or lose the cottage?"

Tally nodded, her expression turning serious. "Of course, I remember."

"Well, something incredible just happened. A woman—Susan Green—came to see me. Her mother, Linda, was a close friend of Nana's years ago. Apparently, Nana deeded Linda a house when her husband left her alone with no money and a small child. She even gave Linda some funds to start her own business."

Tally's eyes widened in surprise. "Genevieve was always so generous. She had a heart of gold."

"And guess what? Genny Cosmetics—you've heard of them?"

Tally nodded.

"The company is named after Nana. Her friend, Linda, founded the company."

"Wow, that's quite a story."

"And that's how it comes back to me and Nana's cottage. Susan told me that Linda recently passed away, and on her deathbed, she told Susan about Nana's kindness and asked Susan to repay that debt by giving me the proceeds from the sale of the house Nana deeded to her mother."

Tally gasped, her hand flying to her mouth. "That's wonderful! How much are we talking about?"

She grinned, barely able to contain her excitement. "Enough to save the cottage, Tally. It's more than enough to pay off the loan and keep Nana's home in the family." She twirled around in happiness. "Don't you see? This means I can stay."

Tally wrapped her in a tight hug. "Oh, I'm so happy for you! Didn't I tell you that Belle Island had a way of making things work out?"

Evie hugged her back. "There's just one small catch," she said as they pulled apart. "The funds are tied up in some estate mess right now because of some issue with the trust Linda set up. But Susan assured me it should be resolved any day."

Tally squeezed her hands. "The important thing is that you have hope now. I'm certain the cottage will be saved, and it's all thanks to your grandmother's kindness coming back to you."

She nodded as a sense of peace settled over her. "You're right. Nana always believed in the power of kindness and generosity. Even though she's gone, her love is still protecting me and the cottage."

Tally smiled, her eyes misty with emotion. "Your grandmother's legacy lives on. And now, you get to continue that legacy by keeping her cottage and her memory alive."

"I'm so happy. I can't believe it."

Tally's eyes twinkled with excitement. "You know who else would be thrilled to hear this news? Randy. You should go tell him right away."

Her heart skipped a beat. She hadn't spoken to him since their argument, and the thought of facing him now made her nervous. "I don't know, Tally. We didn't exactly part on the best terms. And… there's still the chance the funds won't come through in time."

"They will." Tally nodded emphatically.

"Okay, maybe I will talk to him."

But as she walked back to the cottage, her courage faded. She'd wait to talk to him until after she was sure she was getting the funds. Because if it all fell through, she couldn't bear to crush him again.

Evie took a long walk that evening, trying to settle her nerves. So much had happened in the last few weeks, the last few days. Now the very real possibility that she could stay here on the island was just within her grasp.

She finally turned around and headed back to the cottage as the sky was just beginning to put on a showy sunset. As she looked down the beach, she saw a lone person walking toward her.

She sucked in a deep breath. No, that

couldn't be Randy, could it? But as they neared each other, she saw that it was.

It wasn't like she could avoid him standing out here in the open on the beach. She knew the minute he realized it was her, because he stopped in his tracks, looked back behind him, and then just stood there.

She took another deep breath, then closed the distance between them. "Hey," she said, not really knowing what else to say.

"Hi." He looked at her quickly, then trained his gaze on the waves.

Maybe this was a sign she should tell him her news. The news Tally had encouraged her to tell him.

Her heart raced as she stood before Randy. The crash of waves echoed in her ears, almost drowning out the sound of her own rapid breathing. She searched his face for any sign of softening, but his expression remained impassive, and he kept his arms crossed tightly over his chest.

"Randy, I…" she began, her voice wavering. "I need to tell you something important."

He gave a slight nod, his gaze fixed somewhere over her shoulder.

She gathered her courage. "A woman

named Susan came to see me yesterday. She's the daughter of someone my grandmother helped years ago."

His eyebrows lifted slightly, but he remained silent.

"It turns out," she continued, her words tumbling out faster now, "that my grandmother deeded a house to Susan's mother, Linda. They've just sold it, and Susan says it was her mother's wish to give me the proceeds to repay Nana for her kindness."

She paused, watching Randy's face for any reaction. His jaw tightened, but he said nothing.

"The thing is," she pressed on, "there's some legal issue with the trust Linda set up. The money's tied up in court right now. But Susan said any day the funds will come through."

Still no reaction.

"I might be able to stay after all. To keep the cottage. There's a really good chance."

Randy's stoic expression faltered for a moment, a flicker of something—hope? doubt?—passing across his features.

She stepped closer. "I know you were hurt when I said I was leaving. I was so overwhelmed by the thought of losing the cottage and someone else living in it. And then that job came up. I didn't mean to hurt you. But now, don't you see? There's a really good chance I can stay."

He stood there staring at her, but said nothing.

"I—I just wanted you to know."

She waited, the silence stretching between them punctuated only by the rhythmic crash of waves on the shore.

He finally spoke. "That's great about the cottage, really it is. Miss G would be pleased."

She held her breath, waiting for him to continue.

"But it really doesn't change the fact that your first instinct was to run away. You chose to leave. You didn't choose… me."

His words stung, cutting deep into her heart. She'd been so focused on the practical aspects of staying—keeping the cottage and finding a way to make it work financially—that she hadn't fully considered the emotional impact her initial decision to leave had on him.

"Randy, I…" The words caught in her throat. What could she say? He was right. Of course he was upset. His wife had left him, then she'd chosen to leave. It didn't matter that she thought she *had* to leave. It still hurt him.

She looked out at the waves, trying to gather her thoughts. The sun was sinking lower on the horizon, painting the sky in brilliant hues of orange and pink with just a splattering of purple.

It was the kind of dazzling sunset a person wanted to share with someone.

Turning back to Randy, she saw the hurt in his eyes, the rigid set of his jaw. She realized that her decision to leave hadn't just been about the cottage or the job. It had been about him too, about the connection they'd made and the potential for something more.

"You're right," she admitted softly. "I didn't choose you. I was scared and overwhelmed. I took… the easy way out. I'm sorry. But Randy, that doesn't mean I don't care about you."

She took a step closer to him, her heart pounding. "Can't you forgive me?"

His face softened only slightly. "I forgive you. I know you did what you thought you had to do. But… it still doesn't change things between us. I can't…" He shook his head. "I just can't."

And with that, he turned around and walked away with the sunset flaunting its presence behind her, mocking her standing alone on the beach.

CHAPTER 19

Evie struggled through the next days, torn between packing up the cottage or not. Each day, she waited for news from Susan. Each day got closer and closer to the deadline to pay back Mr. Barlowe.

With the deadline approaching and no news from Susan, she finally got the boxes out and started packing. Soon she had a neat stack of packed boxes in the corner. Then another stack.

Her phone rang, and she snatched it off the table, seeing from the caller ID that it was Susan. "Hello?" Her voice was a mix of apprehension and hope.

"Evie, hi. I'm just checking in. My lawyer is working on it and still says it will be any day."

Her heart plummeted. Not the news she was

hoping for. "Oh… I only have two more days. I guess it might not come in time after all."

"I'm sorry, Evie. I know my lawyer is doing everything he can."

The thought of losing Nana's cottage after she'd been so close to keeping it crushed her. She turned around slowly, taking in the tiny details. The ring holder by the kitchen sink where Nana took off her wedding rings to do dishes. The foldout stool in the corner that Nana used to reach the higher shelves. The worn table where they had done so many jigsaw puzzles. She closed her eyes.

"Are you okay?" Susan's voice interrupted her stream of memories.

"I will be." Her voice caught. Though this time it would take quite a bit for her to recover —if she ever did.

"I'm so sorry. I'll keep trying."

Susan hung up and Evie turned to start packing more boxes as her heart clutched in actual pain from the knowledge that she'd lost everything. The cottage with its wonderful memories, a chance to stay on Belle Island, and… Randy.

~

Randy entered Magic Cafe, hoping that a good meal might improve his mood. But he doubted it. He took a table inside instead of one out by the beach like he preferred. But out there was where he sat with Evie. He needed a change.

Tally came out and set down a menu. Not that he needed one. He had the menu memorized by now. "Afternoon."

"Hey, Tally."

She looked at him closely. "I thought you'd be in a better mood when you heard the news that Evie might not have to leave."

He let out a long sigh. "I heard. But it really doesn't make a difference."

"What do you mean? Don't you want her to stay? I thought you two had feelings for each other. Or at the very least, the start of something."

"We did. But then she chose to leave. I don't know why I even ever let myself get involved with her."

Tally let out a gentle laugh. "Of course you do. Because she is a wonderful woman. Generous like her grandmother. And I know she misses you."

He looked up at her. "Tally, I just can't. I can't take a chance that she'll leave me just like my ex-wife. And she already chose leaving over me. Her chance of staying here won't change that fact."

"Randy, I adore you, and I say this with love. You're being a fool." Tally shook her head. "Don't let that ex-wife of yours ruin your future. You're letting what she did influence all your choices. Don't give her that hold over you."

He stared at Tally, surprised by her tough love.

She continued, "And can't you see how hard this was on Evie? Look at it from her side. First, she lost her beloved Nana, then she finally decided to stay, *then* found out about the loan. She was losing the cottage she loved, and she got a job offer back home. It was the practical decision to make to go back home."

"But I wanted her to pick me," he admitted softly.

"Then give her a reason to. Tell her how you feel about her. Give her a reason to stay, even if she loses the cottage and has no job. Take a chance. Ask her to stay." Tally pinned him with a stare. "You sometimes have to risk it all for love."

CHAPTER 20

Randy's heart pounded as he paced back and forth on the porch of Evie's cottage. He wiped his sweaty palms on his shorts, trying to summon the courage to knock. Tally's words rang in his mind, urging him to take a chance. But what if he told Evie how he felt and asked her to stay and she still rejected him?

He took a deep breath and raised his hand to knock, then lowered it again. This was ridiculous. He was acting like a nervous teenager. He was a grown man, for Pete's sake. He should be able to have a simple conversation with a woman he cared about. And he did care about her. A lot.

Before he could change his mind again, he rapped his knuckles against the wooden door.

He held his breath as he waited, straining to hear any movement inside. Maybe she wasn't home. Maybe this was a sign he shouldn't—

The door swung open, and there she was, looking unbelievably beautiful even with a smudge of dirt on her cheek. Her eyes widened in surprise, then a flicker of hope crossed her face before her expression turned neutral.

"I… wasn't expecting you."

He opened his mouth to speak, but the words caught in his throat. He cleared it and tried again. "Evie, I… Can we talk? Please?"

She hesitated for a moment. Finally, she nodded and stepped back. "Come in."

He followed her into the living room, his eyes immediately drawn to the boxes lined up in neat stacks around the room. Other boxes stood open and waiting to be filled. His stomach clenched at the sight.

They stood facing each other, an awkward silence stretching between them. He shoved his hands in his pockets, not sure what to do with them. She crossed her arms over her chest.

"I'm sorry," they both blurted out at the same time.

He let out a small laugh, some of the tension easing from his shoulders. "Let me go first." He took a deep breath. "First, I'm sorry for how I reacted when you told me about leaving. I shouldn't have gotten angry. I should have tried to understand your position better."

Her expression softened. "And I'm sorry for not fighting harder to stay. For not considering your feelings more."

They fell silent again, the air between them thick with unspoken words and emotions.

He gathered his courage and took a step closer to her. "I… I don't want you to go. I know it's selfish of me to ask, especially with everything that's happening with the cottage. But I can't bear the thought of you leaving."

Her eyes widened. "Randy, I—"

"Please, let me finish," he said gently. "I know I hurt you by pushing you away. The truth is, I was scared. My ex-wife left me, and I've been afraid to open my heart again. But being with you… it's made me realize that some things are worth the risk."

He reached out and took her hand in his. "I can't promise it'll be easy. We both have our own baggage to deal with. But I want to try, Evie. I want to see where this could go. Will you stay? Will you give us a chance? Even if everything falls through with the cottage, will you stay?"

He paused and looked deep into her eyes. "Choose me, Evie. Stay for me, stay *with* me. Choose me."

Evie stood looking at Randy, unable to tear her gaze away from his face. His eyes were filled with a mix of hope and vulnerability, and she could see the depth of his feelings for her. In that moment, everything became clear. She knew where she belonged, and it was right here, with Randy.

She took a deep breath and said, "I choose you, Randy. I want to stay."

"Even if things don't work out with the cottage?"

"Even if that happens. I want to stay on Belle Island with you."

The words had barely left her lips before she launched herself into his arms. He wrapped them around her, holding her close as if he never wanted to let go. She buried her face in his chest, breathing in his familiar scent, feeling the warmth of his embrace.

"And I choose you, Evie," he whispered against her, his voice thick with emotion. "I promise we'll make it work."

Tears of joy and relief streamed down her face as she clung to him. All the uncertainty and fear that had plagued her melted away in the face of his support and love.

"I'm sorry I ever considered leaving," she said, pulling back to look into his eyes. "I was just so scared of losing the cottage, of not having a plan. But I realize now that none of that matters as much as being with you."

He cupped her face in his hands, his thumbs gently wiping away her tears. "I understand. I'm sorry I couldn't see it from your perspective before. I was just so afraid of losing you. Of you leaving me."

She leaned into his touch, relishing the feeling of his rough, calloused hands against her skin. "You won't lose me. I'm here to stay, no matter what happens with the cottage."

He smiled, his eyes crinkling at the corners in the way she loved. "We'll figure it out together. I promise."

She nodded, her heart swelling with love and gratitude. She fiercely wanted to stay here in the cottage, but if she couldn't, at least she would be with Randy, where she belonged.

She looked up at him, her heart swelling with happiness. "Say, how about we open another item from the Christmas box? I think it's getting a little lonely without us."

He grinned at her. "Then I think we should open another one."

They sat on the couch, close together, as she chose another item. "There's only one left after this one," she said as she carefully unwrapped the one she'd chosen.

She broke into a smile as she unfolded the paper. It was an old crayon picture she'd drawn when she was just a child. It showed her and Nana—in very rough stick figures—standing on the beach with a pail between them. The lighthouse towered above them—slightly crooked. Her signature was scrawled in the corner. "I can't believe she kept this all these years."

"Of course she did. She loved you so very much." Randy squeezed her hand.

"And I loved her just as much."

CHAPTER 21

Randy came over to her cottage bright and early on the day the debt was due to be paid. She'd heard from Mr. Barlowe that he'd come by first thing this morning. Her heart was breaking at all she was losing, softened only by knowing that even without the beloved cottage, she still had Randy.

He stepped inside, carrying a box from The Sweet Shoppe. "Figured we'd have some breakfast while we wait."

"It's that or pack more boxes." She motioned to a half dozen boxes still open on the floor, half-packed. "I assume he won't kick me out today. Though, maybe he will?"

"No matter what happens, I'm here for

you." he squeezed her hand as they went into the kitchen.

She poured them coffee, and they put the cinnamon rolls on plates. The familiar sharing of breakfast that she'd come to love now felt more like their last meal. She tried to keep up her part of the conversation and choke down some bites of breakfast.

A brisk knock sounded at the door. Loud. Insistent. That had to be Mr. Barlowe. She rose, and Randy followed her to the door. With a deep breath for courage, she opened it.

Mr. Barlowe stood there, his face a bit red and his eyes showing a hint of anger.

"Good morning, Mr. Barlowe. Do you want to come in?" she said politely. Well, almost politely.

"No, this will do." He barked the words. "I don't know how you did it." He looked over her shoulder, gazing bitterly into the cottage. "Like I said, I don't know how you did it, but the loan is paid off."

"I—I don't understand," she stammered, confused.

"I don't either." Mr. Barlowe's face flushed a deeper red, his voice clipped, barely concealing his anger. "My lawyer just called and said the loan was paid. We have no claim on the cottage."

"You—don't?" Her heart beat faster and faster, each beat echoing in her ears, afraid to believe this was true. "How?"

"I have no idea." His words came out in a growl, his jaw clenched. "I just know it's paid. Here's a signed copy that shows the debt is paid." Mr. Barlowe thrust a paper toward her, crushing it into her hands. "Good day."

He gave one more disgruntled gaze at the cottage, his eyes narrowing as if trying to solve a puzzle. He stomped down the steps. With a grunt of displeasure, he yanked open his car door, slid inside, and slammed the door shut. He peeled away, leaving a cloud of dust in his wake.

She turned to Randy, who stood motionless, looking as stunned as she was. Then, as if emerging from a trance, his features softened into a smile that lit up his entire face. He threw back his head and let out a deep, joyous laugh. He scooped her up in his arms, twirling her around the room. "You did it. You saved Miss G's cottage."

When he finally set her down, she grabbed his arms to steady herself. "But how? How did the loan get paid off?"

He shook his head, his expression a mix of confusion and relief. "Don't look at me. Though if I'd had the money, I would have paid it off in a heartbeat."

She frowned. "It doesn't make any sense."

Another knock sounded at the door and she turned to open it to find Susan standing there. "Susan, what are you doing here?"

Susan's gaze flitted between Randy and her. "I guess you know by now?"

"Know what?"

"That I paid off the loan." Her words tumbled out in a rush. "It was the right thing to do. Mother would have wanted you to keep the cottage. When the estate is settled, you can pay me back."

Her mouth dropped open. "You… you did this for me?"

"Of course. I was in a position to help you, just like Genevieve was in a position to help my mother."

"Oh Susan, I can't thank you enough." She threw her arms around the woman, hugging her tightly.

"There's no need to thank me. Your grandmother saved my mother and helped her start her company." Susan paused for a moment. "And I was at this cute little place, Magic Cafe, for breakfast. Met this charming woman, Tally. When I said I was coming to visit you, we got to chatting. She knew about the loan, so I told her how it had been taken care of. But she did mention you were looking for a job."

Her mind whirled, trying to process everything. "I am, but—I'm in tech and there's not much of that on the island."

"As it turns out, Genny Cosmetics has an opening for cyber security. I did some checking on your background after I was here last. I was just curious." She shrugged. "You've worked at some very impressive jobs. Saw your current resume on the JobNetwork website. The job is yours if you want it. Remote work, of course. I know you won't want to leave the island. There'll be some meetings you'll need to fly in for or we can do video meetings. We'll work it out."

Susan handed her an envelope, and Evie stared at it.

"The job specifics and salary are all in there. Take a few days to think about it and let me know."

She swallowed hard, fighting back tears. Could the day possibly get any better?

"Thank you. That's so generous."

"No, you're very qualified for the job and we've been looking for quite a while for someone for this position. The internet is a bit crazy these days. We want it safe for our customers to shop online, and we want the strongest security with any information they give us."

It did sound like a job that was made for her skill set.

Susan bent down and picked up a box by her feet. "These are some things I found in the house before we sold it. From your grandmother's family. I thought you'd like to have them."

"Thank you." She took the box.

"I'm heading out now. Need to get back home. Still have a bunch of holiday preparations to take care of, plus our company Christmas party." Susan gave her another warm hug. "I'm so grateful that my mother and your grandmother were such close friends, and that we've had the chance to meet. I really hope we can become more than just coworkers—I'd love for us to be friends."

Susan stepped back, giving a final smile before she left. As the door closed softly behind her, she turned to Randy, her eyes wide with disbelief. "That was just… incredible. I'm still trying to process everything that just happened."

"It was."

"And I was just thinking this day couldn't get any better."

"Oh, I bet it can." His eyes sparkled with mischief as he took the box from her hands. He set it down and turned to her, pulling her gently into his arms.

He lowered his lips to hers in a tender kiss, as soft as a whisper, filled with unspoken emotion. The world faded away as their hearts beat in rhythm. The kiss was everything she'd ever imagined and more.

When they finally parted, she grinned up at him. "You're right. That absolutely did make the day better."

CHAPTER 22

The next morning, Randy came over to help her unpack and put everything away that she wanted to keep. He tirelessly hauled off boxes marked for donation to the various charities around town while making trips to the local dump with items that were beyond salvaging.

As they tackled the living room, Evie carefully arranged her beloved books back onto the shelves, their familiar spines bringing a feeling of home to the cottage. All the books were back where they belonged, except for some that she donated to the library, knowing they would find new readers to enjoy them.

"I'm glad I didn't pack up the kitchen yet," she admitted as they paused for a well-deserved break. Settling down at the worn kitchen table, they sipped glasses of sweet tea. "I should have, but I couldn't bring myself to do it."

"It's one less room we have to put back together." He smiled and raised his glass, the ice jingling against the sides.

"I needed to go through Nana's things, anyway. So at least that's finished. Now I just have to figure out where to put everything back."

"Good thing you have such a handsome helper." He winked at her, his eyes twinkling.

A smile tugged at her lips. "Oh, the handsomest."

The lighthearted moment stretched between them, comfortable and familiar.

Randy set his glass down and nodded toward the counter. "Is that the box from Susan?"

"It is. Let's look at what's in it while we sit here." She grabbed the box and set it on the table. She lifted the lid and peered inside. On top was an old Bible. She carefully took it out and opened it. There, on the first page, was a family tree. She scanned down the names and gasped when she came to two of them. "Look. It's Fred and Lula. They got married—" She looked up, grinning. "On March 2, 1908. The music box must have been a wedding present."

"I guess we solved the mystery of another item from the Christmas box." He smiled in satisfaction. He leaned over to examine the family tree carefully, tracing his finger along the lines connecting generations. "It looks like Fred might have been Miss G's great-uncle?"

"Really? So that's why she had the music box." She picked up a stack of old photos, sifting through them, and recognized Nana and Linda in many of them.

He selected a stack of brittle papers from the box and carefully leafed through them, the soft rustle filling the kitchen. Suddenly, he paused and let out a warm chuckle as he handed a page to her. She took it, her eyes scanning the faded ink before a smile spread across her face. "Oh my goodness, Randy. Nana inherited the house in Plymouth from Fred and Lula. It's like pieces of a puzzle falling into place. It all comes full circle, doesn't it?"

"It does indeed," he agreed, his eyes twinkling with their shared discovery.

She tapped her fingers on the worn table and frowned. "So the only thing we haven't figured out is who helped Sam Waterman save his glass-blowing business. That's still a mystery."

"There's still the question of why Miss G had that piece of sea glass that looks like a Christmas tree, too."

"Well, we figured out most of the items from the box. What do you say we open the last one on Christmas Day? Just like I used to do with the advent calendar Nana made."

"I think that's a great idea."

She set the paper down and leaned back in her chair. "You know what I was thinking?"

"Nope, but I bet you're going to tell me." He winked at her, a smile settling onto his lips.

"I think we should have a big open house here on Christmas Eve. Invite everybody. I'm just so grateful to have the chance to become part of this town, live on this island."

"Can we make more of Miss G's cookies for the party?" A boyish grin spread across his face.

She smiled at him. "Yes, I'm sure that could be arranged."

CHAPTER 23

Bing Crosby's smooth voice filtered through Evie's cottage on Christmas Eve. She carefully checked the table full of Christmas cookies, punch, and appetizers. All made from recipes she found in Nana's recipe box. Her gaze darted over to the clock on the wall, checking the time as panic ran through her that no one would show up.

Randy came in from the deck, where he had been making sure the Christmas lights were perfect. He walked inside, grinning. "I still say you should have let me put up one more string."

"Santa is sure to be able to find this cottage. It's like a landing strip out there." She laughed. "Okay, not quite, but it does have a nice warm light out there if people want to wander outside." She glanced at the clock yet again.

"Don't worry." He nudged her gently. "They'll be here. All of them."

As if on cue, the doorbell rang—finally—and she went to answer it. Soon the cottage filled up with people.

Tally came over and gave her a hug. "I love seeing Genevieve's cottage all decorated for Christmas. She loved the holidays so."

"She did. Oh, and you know that Christmas box of Nana's I told you I found? I've been opening up the items in it one by one. And I've figured out the history of most of the items and why Nana might have kept them. There's still a bit of a mystery around a glass-blown ornament she kept though. I know it was made by Sam Waterman, a man who owned a small glass-blowing business here on the island. He almost lost his business during the depression. But rumor has it some kind person got in touch with a big department store chain and they put in a large order and it saved his business. I wasn't able to figure out who did it though."

Tally's expression softened, her eyes warm with memories. She leaned in closer, her voice lowering to a conspiring whisper. "I can answer that for you. But it's not really known around town. It was my grandfather."

"Really?" Nothing about this town truly surprised her anymore. It seemed everyone was interconnected.

"Yes. He wanted to help Sam out, and my grandfather went to school with someone in the upper levels of management of the department store. But he never wanted anyone to know it was him. He did it to be kind, not for any acclaim. Can you keep his secret?"

"Yes, of course I will. But thank you for telling me. He's like Nana, helping people quietly, behind the scenes, not for the recognition."

"Did you figure out all the rest of the items?" Tally tilted her head, her expression curious.

"All except for a pretty piece of sea glass. I guess she just might have kept it because it was so unusual."

Tally's lips curved into a smile. "Let me guess. Is it in the shape of a Christmas tree?"

Her eyes widened. "It is. How did you know?"

"Genevieve and William found it right on the beach in front of Magic Cafe one Christmas morning. They showed it to me. He asked her to marry him that day."

Her heart flooded with warmth as she realized what a special memory it held for Nana. And now for her.

Tally drifted off to mingle in the crowd, her laughter blending in with the cheerful hum of conversation. Randy made his way over, slipping his arm around her waist. "Looks like your first party is a big success."

"It is. And I found out more about our mystery items." As she told him what Tally had revealed, his face lit up in amazement.

"Well, it looks like we've been successful with all the items." He smiled down at her, his eyes warm with affection.

"As long as we're lucky with tomorrow's item."

"We will be. I just have a feeling." He tightened his arm reassuringly around her waist, his words carrying a certainty she found it impossible not to believe.

She leaned against him, enjoying his warmth, enjoying having him here to share this night with her.

A steady stream of townspeople came in and out for hours. Their warm greetings and genuine enthusiasm for her decision to stay wrapped around her in a welcoming embrace. They showered her with compliments on Nana's cookies and how cute the cottage looked, decorated for Christmas just like Nana had done.

Finally, the last guest left, and she sank onto the couch. "That was lovely. I can't believe how many people came. And they were so nice to me."

"Of course they were. They're happy you're staying here." Randy settled beside her. "You're part of the island now. You're home."

She swept her gaze around the cottage, taking in the subtle changes that had made it her own, with plenty of Nana's influence still evident. Her own things mingling with Nana's.

With a startling clarity, she realized it did feel like home now. Especially with Randy right here beside her.

CHAPTER 24

The next morning, Evie flung open the door to Randy's knock, excited to see him and share Christmas morning with him. He swept her up in a hug, then set her down and kissed her. She grinned up at him. "That's a nice way to start a day."

"Merry Christmas, Evie." His fingers lightly brushed away a wayward strand of hair away from her face. "I can't imagine spending Christmas without you. I'm glad you stayed."

A rush of contentment flooded through her. "I am too." She squeezed his hands. "Now, let's go open the last item in the Christmas box. I can't wait any longer."

They settled on the couch with the box resting between them. He gave her an encouraging smile as she slowly opened the lid, plunging her hand inside to grasp the last item. She took it out and unwrapped it, gasping as she saw what she held in her hands—a delicate silver bracelet with tiny pieces of light-colored sea glass embedded in it.

She looked up at Randy. "Nana gave this to me when I was a little girl. It was my Belle Island bracelet. I only wore it when I came here to the island. It made it… more special to me. Like a secret Nana and I shared."

He slipped it onto her wrist and she stared at it, feeling a strong connection to Nana, to the cottage, to the island. Suddenly an idea struck her and she jumped up, tugging on Randy's hand. "Come on, there's somewhere we need to go."

He got up agreeably and followed her outside. "Headed anywhere in particular?"

"The lighthouse," she said, as if it was the most logical place to go on Christmas morning.

They walked along the edge of the water, the only people on the long stretch of sand. It was just the two of them, the birds soaring above, and the waves racing up to greet them. The pink tint of sunrise faded to a brilliant blue sky filled with fluffy clouds.

They walked on until they reached the lighthouse and stood at its base, facing the vast expanse of the sea. A gentle breeze tousled her hair and stroked her skin. She couldn't ask for a more perfect morning.

A flash of teal caught her gaze, and she pointed. "What's that? Just out there at the edge of the waves."

He took a few steps into the water and reached down, scooping it up before returning and handing it to her.

"Oh, look." She stared at it in awe. "It's sea glass… and it looks like a heart, doesn't it?"

He looked closely. "It does."

She clenched it tightly in her hands. "You know what I'm going to do with this?"

"What?"

"I'm going to put it in Nana's Christmas box. A reminder of this Christmas. Our first Christmas."

"Our first of many." He pulled her into a hug. "I think that's a wonderful idea. This has certainly been a Christmas I'll never forget."

"It has, hasn't it?" She looked up at him, all her emotions raw and near the surface. So much had happened since she'd returned to the island.

"And I have something I want to give you for Christmas," he said softly.

"What's that?" She looked up into the depths of his eyes, and it was as if she could feel his emotions intertwining with hers.

"It's more something I want you to know..." He reached out and cupped her chin, tilting her face up, locking his gaze with hers. "I love you, Evie. You make me feel whole. Like where I belong is right here with you."

Her heart beat in double time, and the love she felt for him—and had tried to ignore—swelled through her, commanding her attention. "I love you too." She managed to whisper the words before the gentle sea breeze took them away, flinging them across the water, announcing their love to the world.

He leaned down and captured her lips, a gentle kiss full of love and promise. She stood there in his arms, where she belonged, and it was like the last piece of her heart fell into place. And she'd treasure the heart-shaped sea glass they'd found as a reminder of the day they both admitted their love.

As they stood on the shoreline, the waves washed a tiny yellow shell up to their feet. Randy glanced down at it and smiled. "You know about the legend of the lighthouse? If you make a wish and throw a shell into the sea, your wish will come true?"

"Of course I do. I've made many wishes here. And I've made two since I've returned."

Curiosity lit up his face. "Really? What were they?"

"I wished that I could keep the cottage and find a way to live here."

"That wish came true." He brushed a finger along her cheek, smiling gently. "And the other wish?"

"When I first came to the island, I came here to Lighthouse Point." She glanced up at the lighthouse, then back toward Randy. "I was feeling alone and lost. I missed Nana so much." She closed her eyes briefly, reliving those first painful days. "And I stood right here and wished to feel happy again and find joy."

His eyes never left her face. "And did you find it?"

A slow smile spread across her lips as she met his gaze. "I did. Right here. With you."

He kissed her again, there under the familiar, comforting presence of the lighthouse. The yellow shell tumbled down the shore, washing back out to sea. She had no need to make another wish. All hers had come true.

Thank you for reading my story. I hope it brought you a bit of the magic of the Christmas Season. If you want to read more about Belle Island, try my Lighthouse Point series full of family, friendship, and more of the quaint island charm. Learn about the legend of making a wish at Lighthouse Point, and find out more about Tally's story. She's one of my favorite characters!

As always, thanks for reading my stories. I truly appreciate all my readers.

ALSO BY KAY CORRELL

COMFORT CROSSING ~ THE SERIES

The Shop on Main - Book One

The Memory Box - Book Two

The Christmas Cottage - A Holiday Novella (Book 2.5)

The Letter - Book Three

The Christmas Scarf - A Holiday Novella (Book 3.5)

The Magnolia Cafe - Book Four

The Unexpected Wedding - Book Five

The Wedding in the Grove (crossover short story between series - Josephine and Paul from The Letter.)

LIGHTHOUSE POINT ~ THE SERIES

Wish Upon a Shell - Book One

Wedding on the Beach - Book Two

Love at the Lighthouse - Book Three

Cottage near the Point - Book Four

Return to the Island - Book Five

Bungalow by the Bay - Book Six

Christmas Comes to Lighthouse Point - Book Seven

CHARMING INN ~ Return to Lighthouse Point

One Simple Wish - Book One

Two of a Kind - Book Two

Three Little Things - Book Three

Four Short Weeks - Book Four

Five Years or So - Book Five

Six Hours Away - Book Six

Charming Christmas - Book Seven

SWEET RIVER ~ THE SERIES

A Dream to Believe in - Book One

A Memory to Cherish - Book Two

A Song to Remember - Book Three

A Time to Forgive - Book Four

A Summer of Secrets - Book Five

A Moment in the Moonlight - Book Six

MOONBEAM BAY ~ THE SERIES

The Parker Women - Book One

The Parker Cafe - Book Two

A Heather Parker Original - Book Three

The Parker Family Secret - Book Four

Grace Parker's Peach Pie - Book Five

The Perks of Being a Parker - Book Six

BLUE HERON COTTAGES ~ THE SERIES

Memories of the Beach - Book One

Walks along the Shore - Book Two

Bookshop near the Coast - Book Three

Restaurant on the Wharf - Book Four

Lilacs by the Sea - Book Five

Flower Shop on Magnolia - Book Six

Christmas by the Bay - Book Seven

Sea Glass from the Past - Book Eight

MAGNOLIA KEY ~ THE SERIES

Saltwater Sunrise - Book One

Encore Echoes - Book Two

Coastal Candlelight - Book Three

Tidal Treasures - Book Four

And more to come!

CHRISTMAS SEASHELLS AND SNOWFLAKES SERIES (Standalone books. Read in any order.)

Seaside Christmas Wishes

WIND CHIME BEACH ~ A stand-alone novel

INDIGO BAY ~

Sweet Days by the Bay - Kay's complete collection of stories in the Indigo Bay series

ABOUT THE AUTHOR

Kay Correll is a USA Today bestselling author of sweet, heartwarming stories that are a cross between women's fiction and contemporary romance. She is known for her charming small towns, quirky townsfolk, and the enduring strong friendships between the women in her books.

Kay splits her time between the southwest coast of Florida and the Midwest of the U.S. and can often be found out and about with her camera, taking a myriad of photographs, often incorporating them into her book covers. When not lost in her writing or photography, she can be found spending time with her ever-supportive husband, knitting, or playing with her puppies - a cavalier who is too cute for his own good and a naughty but adorable Australian shepherd. Their five boys are all grown now and while she misses the rowdy boy-noise chaos, she is thoroughly enjoying her empty nest years.

Learn more about Kay and her books at kaycorrell.com

While you're there, sign up for her newsletter to hear about new releases, sales, and giveaways.

WHERE TO FIND ME:
My shop: shop.kaycorrell.com
My author website: kaycorrell.com
authorcontact@kaycorrell.com

Join my Facebook Reader Group. We have lots of fun and you'll hear about sales and new releases first!
www.facebook.com/groups/KayCorrell/

I love to hear from my readers. Feel free to contact me at authorcontact@kaycorrell.com

facebook.com/KayCorrellAuthor
instagram.com/kaycorrell
pinterest.com/kaycorrellauthor
amazon.com/author/kaycorrell
bookbub.com/authors/kay-correll

Made in the USA
Monee, IL
11 June 2025